No Truce

With The Furies

⚜   ⚜   ⚜

A Collection

Of Short Stories

By

Noah W. Newmann

2023

No Truce
With The Furies

Noah W. Newmann

This book is a collection of original short stories. Any resemblances to current events or locales, or to persons, living or dead, is entirely unintentional and a product of the author's imagination.

This edition contains the complete text
of the original works.

NOT ONE WORD HAS BEEN OMITTED

No Truce
With The Furies:
A Collection

2023 Hollingsworth/Scott Paper*cut*

Edited by Katherine V. Pioch & W. Scott Newmann Jr.

PUBLISHING HISTORY

First Edition / October 2023 by Hollingsworth/Scott
Set in EB Garamond

*All rights reserved
Copyright © 2023 Noah W. Newmann*

ISBN: 9798866158898

Printed in USA by 48HrBooks (www.48HrBooks.com)

No part of this book may be reproduced or transmitted in any form or by any means, electronic or mechanical, including photocopying, recording, or by any information storage or retrieval system, without permission in writing from the publisher. For information, address all inquiries to: Noah. W. Newmann 1845 East Northgate Dr. Irving, Texas 75062 #337. Or to wspapercut@outlook.com.

Contents

Dedication 3

A Stop at Wigley's 5

Did Your Lips Say Amen? 27

Otis 35

Pickett's Field 59

Over 71

Revelations 75

The Crossroads at Oldforge Gibbet 103

An Interesting Hypothesis 109

Le Révolutionnaire 117

It Was Easier 131

No Truce With The Furies
A Collection

Hollingsworth/Scott Paper*cut*

NOAH W. NEWMANN

No Truce With The Furies

This book is dedicated to Mom & Dad, who are my two best friends, supported me in my artistic efforts, and offered the best encouragement and critiques a son could hope for.

Thank You.

Noah W. Newmann

The furies are at home / in the
mirror; it is their address.
There is no truce / with the furies.

From "Reflections" by
R. S. Thomas

A Stop at Wigley's

ELIJAH WIGLEY KEPT HIMSELF to himself and did not often speak his mind. Wigley would sit on the wooden bench of his gas station, a twist of chew tucked behind his lip, with his hat pulled low and boots splayed, listening to the tinny play of music that came from the garage's radio.

His eyes roamed the road that stretched past fields of fallow farm. Along this road, the farmers and tenants had left after the first years of drought. No rain meant no crops to harvest, which meant no money in the bank. Many left in their rattletrap cars, entire lives roped onto the tops of their cabs. They left the gray farmhouses that were like boxy tombstones at the edge of their fields.

Each family went in search of their own promised land. Even the local preacher had left. The scattering of houses and barns and meeting places that dared to call itself a town, fixed around that toothpick steeple of the church, began to lose itself to the country. The prairie poured steadily into town, through the windows and doors and porches of the barns, pushing in at the side streets and down the backways so that the homesteads fell into drifts of dust. What was left of the trees lining the streets and byways were faded now and withered into frail, shivering ghosts with bark turned pale as a cadaver's skin.

Banks of puffy white clouds and flashes of heat lightning had taunted the bent heads of travelers, seeming at first to promise rain, but never a drop fell. Back and forth, like smoke from a grassfire, the clouds would swing out from the level pan of the prairie, towing their shadows behind them.

Wigley's Gas and Oil was at the edge of town. It had two ancient, rickety pumps underneath an old tin canopy that was painted a once cheery red. A garage was attached to a two-story home behind the canopy. A brownish gray stain of dirt was creeping up the edges of the white clapboard, but there were scrub marks where the owners had obviously been at work to keep up appearances. Not many drove that way anymore, but those who did always stopped there.

And all day, Elijah Wigley would sit there.

This was how he was found when Mr. Lamb pulled up under the awning in a bee-yellow pickup, whose bed was filled with bric-a-brac. Mr. Lamb stomped his foot on the clutch and turned the key so that the engine died in a flutter of noise. Fuel gurgled through the entrails of his truck before it leaked through the rusty bottom, drip-dripping into a growing puddle between the tires. Its rhythm was a syncopation behind the Big Band that dribbled out of the shop radio.

Mr. Wigley stood up and reached for the pump.

Mr. Lamb stepped out of the cab of his truck.

"Don't trouble yourself, sir," he said. "I'm a mechanic, and I pump gas. 'Sides I wanna do it myself. Get in, get out real easy."

Mr. Wigley shrugged and sat down.

Mr. Lamb was squat and bull-like, with a bulbous nose and stubby fingers that were used to long work hours and even longer days. His nails were all peeled, like he had been biting them, so he tucked them safely into the front of his green coveralls as if he were ashamed of them.

"Sure is hot, sir," said Mr. Lamb. He took off his ballcap and slapped the dust from his knees. A dark line ran along his forehead where the sweat line had protected his dark skin from turning into something like ash or pewter. "Is there any rain up in those clouds there? Or is God just playin' a trick on us?" Mr. Lamb chuckled as he sauntered over to the bench, which was firmly in the shade. Compared to the sun-blasted landscape, it was the color of pitch.

Wigley nodded slowly, like a man in a doze. "It can feel like that sometimes. I'm Wigley, by the way."

"Mr. Lamb's the name."

"A pleasure." Mr. Wigley watched a dust devil dance into the field on the other side of the road. The clouds overhead encroached, immense.

"This the price o' gas?" asked Mr. Lamb, pointing to the card on the side of the first pump.

Wigley nodded.

"Well, I'll be damned, Wigley. You sure drive a hard bargain."

"Mm." Wigley spat into the dust. There was something to be said for being the only fuel pump for nearly fifty miles.

Mr. Lamb opened up the door to his cab and looked for some coins to slot into the pump. Wigley turned his head to look at his customer.

"Goin' east?"

"You bet."

"Most people goin' west," said Wigley, turning back to the play of dust in the field opposite.

"Most people is idjits, Wigley. You know that. I know that."

Wigley said nothing.

Mr. Lamb counted change in the palm of his hand, then closed the cab again with a metallic clap. He still held his ballcap in one stone-muscled fist while he sorted out the pennies from the nickels.

"I'm headin' east for work," began Mr. Lamb. The coins chinked at the bottom of the receptacle. "It was just time I left home and began afresh, ya know? Sure, I guess you know, bein' all set up ou' here with your pumps and all. Say," he said, squinting up the main street into town. "Where'd all the people go? All I see's those trees that should go up an' down the streets so pretty."

Wigley said nothing.

"I don't see that anythin's open 'tall. Are you the last of 'em Wigley?"

"No, no, sir," came a voice from behind, gentle and feminine. "We ain't the last of 'em by a long shot. It'll take a lot more than drought to drive us out of this place."

Mr. Lamb turned, startled, to see a woman step out from the door of the house. She wiped her hands on an apron that was as wide as her smile. She was tall, like a stork in the way that she walked, with hair as blonde as flax and hands that were always moving. Her eyes twinkled out at the world from a nest of crow's feet.

"Are you the missus?" asked Mr. Lamb, nodding to her. He was not quite certain what to do with himself.

Mrs. Wigley walked past Mr. Lamb and stood behind her husband. "Near everyone moved on west, Mr. Lamb. All's left is a few scattered families on the edge of town. They come by and visit some days." She rested her hands on her husband's shoulders. Her gaze followed Wigley's out over the horizon. "So no, sir. Not ever'one's gone now. There's a few folks left. Every weekend, we go and worship in the church on Sunday, but ever since the preacher left, it's been quite lonesome in there, with the pews gettin' more naked every week, as it were."

"Now ain't that a shame," sighed Mr. Lamb with a shake of his head. He dropped the last bit of his change into the slot. "Preacher up and left, too? That ain't no way fer a preacher to act, no sir."

"Well, our preacher were a very queer man, and a whole sight wiser than most, I tell ya, Mr. Lamb," said Mrs. Wigley, a look of sympathy crossing her face. "I suppose Elijah here didn't tell you how he left us, did he?"

Mr. Lamb shook his head.

"Well..." she said, smiling as if at some private joke. "One Sunday, everyone comes to what they expect to be an ordinary service, bright and early like—This was about four months ago now. Only, when we get there, we find the doors to the church closed. Shut tight with a sign tacked to the door that read, 'He calls me away, so I'm going west. God bless.' That's all he left us. No more preacher, no more regular church, and no more poor box."

"Now ain't that a shame for that preacher, takin' the poor box," mused Mr. Lamb. "But it sure is good of you all to still be gatherin' on Sundays, that's for sure now. Churchin' always does a body good."

Mr. Lamb was not a praying man, but he still shook his head in a show of sympathy. He lifted the nozzle of the pump. He tugged his cap back on, fixed the nozzle into the tank, and pulled the trigger. The pump gurgled, and something inside the tower rattled, followed by the overwhelming stink of gasoline.

"Now what in the blazes—" exclaimed Mr. Lamb. He let go of the trigger and eyed the pump suspiciously.

"There's a kink in the pipin'," said Wigley, shaking his head. He stood up, left an outline of dust on the seat. He walked to the tower pump and kicked it.

"There's been something wrong with the pipin' from the tank to the pump," explained Mrs. Wigley. "It's jus' gone a little cattywampus the last few days is all."

Mr. Lamb scowled at the card on the pump. "I ain't goin' to blow myself up for a few gallons o' gas, an' from the sounds of it, whatever's goin' on downstairs don' sound good 'tall."

He jabbed his finger down, then swept the cap off to run his hand through his hair. Wigley watched him closely, seeing the dark rectangle on the left breast where, ordinarily, a nametag would be stitched into the fabric.

"No sir! I need everythin' intact so I can work. I gotta job east with a cousin o' mine, but he needs a man that can actually hold a socket wrench in his hand, an' if'n I show up to his place all mangled up, he'll take one look at me and say, 'Well, buster, looks like you're sure fire outta luck!' I can't have that, Wigley. You can take yer busted pump and pull on the trigger yourself. I ain't goin' to blow myself up for a few gallons o' gas."

Wigley nodded, scratching his five o'clock shadow. "You a good mechanic?"

Mr. Lamb scowled at Wigley like he had just insulted him. "Shaw, you know I am! I'm a damn sight bettah than anybody here in town, that's for sure."

Wigley put his hands on his hips and looked over Mr. Lamb's shoulder as if he were only incidental to the conversation. He nodded, almost to himself.

"Got yer tools?"

"Sure I do. Right in the back."

"In a rush?"

Mr. Lamb chuckled to himself. He looked once more up the road that stretched eastward.

Telephone poles were posted regularly down the right-hand side of the road, going east—where he should be heading. The black cables bent lazily down, then up again to meet at the blue glass insulators that let Des Moines talk to LA. Mr. Lamb almost heard the businessmen joking with one another in a purr of electricity. Did you hear that one about the Japanese golfer—of course I did, and the one about Wilbur, too—I'll be sure to let my clients know—For sure, and how are the dividends doing?—Like hell. Why do you ask?

Other voices flew out to the cities. They told everyone to keep their ears open, eyes peeled: looking. Even now, Mr. Lamb heard calls being made, underneath all the chatter of business, one department to another, alerting the officers on duty to danger. The sketch artists were taking the descriptions down, outlining a face, filling in the cheekbones, then tacking it up on the WANTED board. All those eyes looking for a scapegoat, someone to blame, someone to hunt.

"Some folks would say that I am in a little bit of a rush, yeah," said Mr. Lamb, looking back toward Wigley. "I can't afford to stop tonight. No sir, I got places to be. But... if'n you want help fixin' up this thing, I can be yer man. I want money back though. An' some more fo' the road."

"All's I can spare is the money," said Wigley. "Money's tight nowadays."

"C'mon, an' go get a screwdriver, an' I'll pry open the money bin myself, take out all I gave, an' no more. I'm a man of my word!" He kicked at the bulging side of one of the pickup's tires.

"Now, Mr. Lamb," said Mrs. Wigley. "We can fix you up a little somethin' extra now, can't we?" She glanced at her husband.

Wigley did not say a word. He considered the ground, numbers almost visibly turning over in his head. Slowly, he dragged his eyes up from the dust and nodded.

"Don't have much in the way of cash money," he said. "But I got some candy bars in the store and some Coke-Colas."

"What kind?"

"Dr. Pepper, RC, and the like."

"RC!" Mr. Lamb laughed. "Now there ya have me, Wigley!"

Mr. Lamb opened the back door to the pickup.

"Well!" he exclaimed and leaned into the bubble of scorching heat to sort through his belongings and get out his toolbox. "If'n that's the case, count me your man, Wigley! We'll set this thing to rights in no time. Sure as hellfire, we got 'er set." Mr. Lamb threw a stained and crusted brown leather shammy into the toolbox before he clapped the lid shut. He stepped back from the cab and closed the door, toolbox dangling from one hand.

"Well, I'm glad to hear it," sighed Mrs. Wigley. "To be honest, that noise was given me the shivers, I tell you. I'm glad you men'll be fixin' it."

Wigley simply stepped forward and extended his hand to Mr. Lamb, who took it with a smile.

"Now point me to where we need to start, and we'll get this a-goin'. We're burnin' daylight." Mr. Lamb let go, and Wigley nodded over toward the garage and the door, which was open, black-mouthed in shadow.

Wigley looked down at the hand with which he had shaken Mr. Lamb's, scowling. He wiped it clean on his overalls that were already spotted with ash and grease, then looked to his wife. Quietly, he shifted his chew from one cheek to the other and followed Mr. Lamb, who was already moving toward the garage.

A pinched crooner's tune crackled like static. Mrs. Wigley fidgeted, her fingers lacing and unlacing as if she were trying to figure out how to solve a jigsaw puzzle. She went into the house to let the men work.

⚜ ⚜ ⚜

"Now, I don't mind the music," ground Mr. Lamb. He let a bolt clatter onto the concrete. "But I sure would like some of that jazz they got playin' from Nawlins. You know the kind, Wigley? Maybe Count Basie or Gene Krupa."

"Mm-hmm."

Mr. Lamb was down in the guts of the piping, legs up to his chest, nestled up under the plexus of hoses that came out of the great-bellied tank. It was cramped in the tank room, and the radio crowded the concrete walls with its music.

"Now I can deal with all o' those big bands, and I like 'em," grunted Mr. Lamb, scooting himself farther down into the crevice so that his belly was only three inches away from the curve of the tank. "But those crooners, Wigley—by God! I can't stand 'em! I jus' can't stand someone who thinks they're what they're not, you know? Same with those singers on the radio. Jus' sing normally for Christ's sake! You know?"

"Mm-hmm."

"I just can't stand a phony," said Mr. Lamb. He worked a wrench, turned a valve. He then pulled his way up into a sitting position, setting the wrench to the side. He squinted at his handiwork and pointed. "Now you see that joint there, Wigley? Up there by the red valve?"

"Mm-hmm."

"I need a... a, uh..."

"Number seven."

"Yeah, yeah, that's the one. The heat's gettin' to my brain, I swear—By God, it's hot." Mr. Lamb wiped his forehead free of sweat and tugged at his ballcap. The air was as thick as pudding down in that room. "Anyway, could you go and fetch that for me?" He looked to the hatch, and Wigley had gone. "And change the music while you're at it!" he called.

There was no answer.

Mr. Lamb looked back at the tank and its series of valves and wheels and gages. His eyes traced the pipe along jointed lines, until he found the valve with its black wheel jutting out at an angle. He nodded to himself, figuring that the line would be safe, and turned the valve. The wheel resisted for a moment before squeaking as the screw turned and rose out of the pipe. The line gurgled and groaned.

Instantly, fuel, stinking and fuming, gushed out, splashing onto his chest, burning his eyes. He swore and quickly turned the wheel clockwise, cutting off the stream. He scrambled to his feet, spitting, retching. Blindly, he reached for the ladder beneath the hatch. The gasoline taste filled his senses so much that he felt as if he were dying. He was a kerosine wick, a fire waiting to happen.

In a rush, he was out of the hatch, his fingers feeling the concrete of the garage floor that was grainy with dust. He scrambled, animal-like on all fours. There was a sink in the corner of the room he had seen, stained with paint and tar, and he tried to open his eyes to see where it was, but the wriggling shadows confused him. Blurred images buried themselves deep in the corners of his eyes like cockleburs, and tears welled but failed to dislodge the chemical darkness. He moved to where he thought he had seen it before. The crooner headed for a crescendo. Mr. Lamb groped for the handle of the sink.

He found it, turned it, and, kneeling with his face in the basin, splashed the tepid water in his eyes. Mr. Lamb let the water run and spat out the taste of oil that made his tongue burn and tingle.

The radio's music snapped off.

Mr. Lamb knelt there, panting and spat into the basin again. He took off his hat and ran his fingers, damp, through his curls.

"Jesus," he muttered to the drain. "Jesus... Jesus have mercy."

Laughter came then, a man's laughter, but pitched high, almost effeminate.

Mr. Lamb looked up from the basin and squinted at the garage door where a silhouette swam up against the pale, evening sky. His eyes smarted, and he turned back to the faucet and scrubbed again. It was Wigley, sure. Mr. Lamb had never heard the man laugh, and it was peculiar for certain, never really what you would expect from someone so silent, but there it was. He scoured his face, hoping what was left of the gasoline would run from his eyes.

"About time you shut off that damn music, Wigley," said Mr. Lamb. "'Bout drove me crazy."

"Now who wouldn't help a friend in need, huh? Who would be so, unkind, and do such a thing, and leave a friend behind?"

It was that voice again, absurdly high, oddly evocative of magnolia trees, wraparound porches, clapboard schools, and Baptist sermons. It was the voice of a southern man, the voice of a planter "up to the big house." It was a voice that gripped Mr. Lamb's throat with icy fingers. It was not Wigley's.

Shuddering, Mr. Lamb looked up from his hands. The water dripped through his fingers and down his wrists, turning the cuffs of his coveralls a dark green. He blinked the remnants of stinging chemicals off his lashes, seeing the silhouette of the man more clearly now. Framed in the doorway, the figure was tall, with shoulders that seemed to hold up the clouds. Now Mr. Lamb knew the laugh, though he did not want to recognize it. He felt his mouth go dry. His tongue stuck between his teeth. The once peaceful quiet in the garage crashed in on his ears now, pressing like a hand on his chest.

Again, the man spoke in his sweet, syrupy tone.

"Did you think that I could or would forget you?" The head tilted to the side, and Mr. Lamb could see the hair, slicked back and shiny. "Please, sir, you insult me... Why, yes, you surely do. To think that you could leave me behind and in such a state... My, my, Mr. Lamb," he lilted. "You got some nerve, and that's for certain. To think that you thought you could leave me behind... It's just sad to see such a man as yourself, a man I once employed, a man I had trusted, take off down that path."

The voice that had been so calm was steadily rising, gaining in volume and weight until it filled the entire garage.

"Speakin' of that, boy... Shouldn't you be gettin' along down the road right about now? I would've thought you'd a been up and gone from here hours ago. Should'a been halfway down to Nashville by now. That's right, boy. You should'a been nice and safe by now... tucked under the sheets of some two-bit roadside hotel, payin' off some throw-a-way white-trash whore with MY MONEY!"

Mr. Lamb ran. He lunged across the shop floor and grabbed for his open toolbox beside the tank room hatch. His feet were caught in the concrete, like dry beach sand, sucking at his heels to drag him down. He ran, clutching the unlatched toolbox to his chest. He floundered and stumbled on his way toward the wide-open door.

"That's right, boy, run! Run on while you can!" shrieked the figure. His voice pitched higher and higher, chasing Mr. Lamb, running him down, like a hound marking a coon, making him blinder than he already was.

The terrified man crashed into Wigley. His toolbox clattered to the ground, scattering tools and nondescript fittings every which way.

"Dammit, dammit!" shouted Mr. Lamb. He scrambled over Wigley, who lay clutching at his chest where the toolbox had struck him.

"What in hell is goin' on, Lamb?"

"I gotta to go, I gotta to go, I gotta to go…!"

"Dammit, boy! What in the hell are you doing?"

"My *God*, get outta my way!"

Laughter was all that Mr. Lamb could hear.

Blind with terror, he scrabbled for the tools which had spilled out of his toolbox. He picked up a hammer at random, a couple of wrenches, and, reaching for a screwdriver, he sliced his hand open on the teeth of a rusting hacksaw blade.

"What on earth?" Mrs. Wigley's voice shrilled into the confusion.

"Outta my way! Outta, my way!"

Mr. Lamb clambered to his feet and pounded toward his rattletrap. Dust gasped up from where his shoes hit the dirt drive. Dumping his armload into the truck bed, he leapt behind the wheel and wrung the starter. Before the driver-side door had shut, the truck's tires were spinning, the vehicle shuddering its way out from the shade of the red-painted canopy and onto the road that stretched out to both horizons.

Mrs. Wigley helped her husband stand. He looked out to the spiral of dust hiding the yellow rattletrap, the roar and sputter of the engine, running on empty, quickly fading into the east.

"What on earth happened?" asked Mrs. Wigley. "Did you say or do something?"

Wigley said nothing. He stood straight and dusted off his knees, all the while scanning the debris Mr. Lamb had left behind. A screwdriver, another shammy stained brown, a spray of washers were scattered over the ground in a trail to the open shop door and beyond. He shook his head, not saying a word and stooped down to pick up the shammy.

As he felt its soft weight in his hand, something rolled out of the oily leather and dropped, shining, onto the concrete. Wigley retrieved it. The music from the shop radio ended abruptly. His wife had enough of the noise.

Looking into his hands, Wigley sighed and glared at the switch-knife with its long, tapering blade and ivory handle. He examined the evil-looking thing and pressed the side-button to close the blade, but it would not move. He turned it in his hands to look at the mechanism. A thick crust of dried brown-black liquid fouled the spring and prevented the blade from yielding to his pressure. It was blood, and it was several days old.

Wigley stared around the garage, then turned slowly to look back at his wife, the stained and stiffened shammy in one hand and the knife in the other. His wife looked at him, lips parted, hands fidgeting. Around them, the ever-moaning voice of the wind was the only sound.

"What's wrong?" asked Mrs. Wigley.

"Nothin'," said Elijah, putting the knife into the shammy and drawing his arm around his wife. "Nothin' 'tall, dear."

A cold wind breathed out from the garage over the Wigleys, and Mrs. Wigley shivered. The two watched a dust devil, as tall as a man, spiral up in the yard. The dust devil turned eastward and moved, steadily, down the road, following the truck.

Evening had come over the station. The sky dimmed as the sun sunk down into the prairie, a shimmering disk of light. On down the highway and a-ways on west, the clouds piled up into the sky, dark and purple, their fat bellies bursting with the promise of rain. But not a drop would they give, only hot wind and thunder to rattle the air.

Noah W. Newmann

Did Your Lips Say Amen?

IT WAS EARLY EVENING, and the tide was running out. The sand and the coral spread under the waves. Above the whitecaps, gulls turned, and their wings touched the sky. The ocean advanced up the beach, then retreated. Advanced, then fell farther into itself.

Clouds came up from the sea and scudded over the horizon in rank upon rank to cover the sky. The clouds gathered themselves as if for a furious sound—but softly, the first drops fell.

It began to rain, and while it rained, the brine that had been tossed on the rocks started to wash away.

The sea, with the hush of the tide, whispered to the beach and the cliffs as it left them: *I love you... I love you... I love you...*

The beach now lay with its knots of coral, the sand spread dead and gray in an endless flat.

On the cliffs above the beach, where the long grass grew, there was a house with a walking path and a garden of purple heather. No light came from that house standing tall and white on the peak of the cliff. The lamp on the porch was dark.

In the upstairs bedroom, light fell through the window, the color of blue velvet. No other color could be made in that gloom. In the seat of the window, on knitted cushions, two sat in naked silence to watch the rolling surf. She looked at him in a moment when the sound of rain slowed and saw him run his hands up then down his legs like he was trying to keep warm. He drew his hands together and worried his fingers. It was a habit he had. He was unhappy, but she was not. She felt a gentleness, the kind that came from him to warm her, something like happiness. She remained in that warmth, letting the quiet pass over them.

He whispered, *"I do love you, you know."* His words made an empty sound, lost in the tapping of rain on the window.

The clock that hung on the opposite wall marked the seconds with a muted, steady tok—tok. Something had happened, she knew. That something was just out of reach, just beyond her field of view, as if it were lingering somewhere, hidden in the half light of the room.

But she did not want to think on that. Not now, not yet. *Let me have this moment,* she prayed silently. *Let me savor the seconds. Let every flavor of time roll over my tongue.* Or, better yet, she could bottle the time up, put it away. Then, when the days grew long, or the nights cold, she could decant this hour and have it again. She craned her head to look out to sea. His words came to her, all merry-go-round in her mind: *I do love you. I do love you. I do—*

"Why did you say that?" she asked.

"What?" He was looking out still, over the cliffs and down onto the flat. A gull had landed on a mound of coral with its orange feet splayed.

"Just asking what you said."

"Oh, right. I was thinking," he began. "...I don't know how I did it, you know? Every year the same, every month over and over. The same old thing... It's honestly kind of ridiculous." The gull skipped over a crag in the coral.

Her warmth began to pass, to fall away, even though she did not want it to go. Skin prickled into gooseflesh all across her. She drew in, clasped her hands around her knees, and watched him, still. The rain pooled on the flat below, the sand running in little creeks down to the sea.

He fiddled with his ring finger.

"I mean," he said, "if you look at it scientifically, the whole contract of marriage—and that's what it is really, a contract, nothing more—it's not a basis for anything good. It only causes pain. In the end, it just doesn't amount to much of anything, scientifically speaking. That's what I was thinking about."

Watching him, she felt a chill.

She followed his gaze. The gull had snapped its beak around a crab. It whipped the creature up, then down onto the coral. Again, it snatched the creature up, not entirely dead, and flung it down, again, then again.

She became aware of her heart beating in her chest, like it had grown to twice its size. It pulled at her and made her breathing shallow.

"What's wrong?" he asked. He looked at her for what seemed like the first time. His eyes were clear and sharp, measuring her every angle.

"Just thinking is all."

"On?"

"When we met."

"And... when was that?"

She looked at him and smiled at the joke. Then she saw it was not a joke.

How could he forget? They met in the arboretum café. She had sold him hot chocolate, and, on the receipt, he had written his number. He was with his daughter, Alexei, on a day trip. Alexei wore her favorite sweater, the one that had been knit specially for her. He later said that he had gotten off early from the office that day and had lost money because of the daytrip, which he did not even want to go on. Little Alexei didn't know about money, could not really know, and had talked about the game on Friday, how she had scored two full runs, and how Mom was making more sweaters for herself and him so that they all could match and be a set.

"You know when," she said, not daring to believe what she already knew to be true.

He watched her for a moment, then looked back out to the gull on the coral. It had begun to pull the legs off the crab.

"Still…" he said, his words retracing old thoughts. "It just doesn't…" and his voice dropped low. *The honey-warmth has left him, too,* she thought, and he rubbed his hands together to keep out the chill.

"What did you say?" she asked once more.

In a whisper, his answer came. *"It can't mean anything."*

She untangled herself, pulling her legs free from his very gently. Her bare feet felt good on the pinewood boards when she walked through the sweet dark, a dark that smelled like salt and oranges.

She stood at the door to the bath and looked back to the window, a hand on the frame.

He sat on the window seat, looking out to sea, slowly running his thumb over the pale band on his ring finger, a tan line from his time in the sun.

His mind wandered, absent from this moment, lost in another.

Why did he remember that day, that hour, that second that stretched into this moment, so unwelcome?

Signing the paper had not been enough for her. She said the love was too large to be bound up by a contract or a certificate. At last, her words compelled him, and he found himself standing before the strange altar, whelmed by that smell of incense. It was a morning service and strangely crowded. To him, it was a contract, but to them, it was something more... To him, he was just checking a box, moving through a ceremony to make her happy, but to her...

He remembered how the light caught the lace of her veil. How the pattern, stitched by a thousand tiny stitches into that shroud, looked like snowflakes drifting down to cover her. In that second, as if she were there beside him, he heard her say the words.

The music of their recessional came to him through the ticking of the clock on the wall and the tapping of the rain on the upstairs window, and suddenly in his mind, he saw only himself sitting there in the evening gloom, his fingers searching, searching for the ring he had hidden. He did not want to think of her, so he had stuck it in the glovebox of his car.

His wife was not there. She was home, watching the time and knitting sweaters in some other evening's gloom. He must remind himself of that. *She was not here. She did not matter. What did he care?* But still... the thought came to him, unbidden, the question that threatened to topple his mind.

"Did you mean it?" he whispered. "*Did you really, really mean it... Did you say it?*"

On the beach, the gull looked up from its meal out over the ocean toward the horizon, a broken shell at its feet.

At the window, his back was turned. At the door of the bath, the woman watched the man fidget with his hands.

She had thought he was beautiful once, and there, in the blue velvet color of the window light, she saw him like that again, like a painting in a museum or statue in a garden. Like those works of art, he had possessed a life, a home for whatever the artist had pulled onto the canvas or drawn out of the granite. She had thought that there had been something good in him, the sort of intangible something that separated him from the rest. But now he had grown cold. She could see it clearly now: Away from the heat, away from the warmth, she saw him for what he truly was.

That hour had a sour taste.

She shivered when she heard him whisper to himself: *"It can't mean anything... It can't..."*

She turned out of the room, her feet still warm on the cold stone floor of the bath, and closed the door behind her.

The door did not slam—but, gently, the latch fell.

On the cliffs outside, where the long grass grew, it was evening.

On the coral, the shell of a crab lay empty.

And on the beach, the tide was running out.

Otis

"WHY CAN'T I GO with you, Grandpa?"

"Because I gotta meet with some old pals o' mine in town."

"But, Grandpa, I promise I'll be quiet."

"No can do, buddy. This meeting is for old folks only."

Grandpa ducked from under the hood of his blue Ford and put his hands against the small of his back to rub at the kink he had complained about all morning. His snow-white eyebrows stuck out as far as his nose.

"Boy! This back'll do me in one day, I tell you."

"But Grandpa..."

"Can't do it, Otis," he said, looking at his grandson with all the pity of an automobile salesman who has just turned down an opening bid. "I'm sorry, but I can't bring you along today. I'll be back before three o'clock. I can promise you that. The boys'll understand. After I get back, we'll go fishing out by the creek where the big bass live." Grandpa smiled his great, magnanimous smile, hands on his hips. "What do you say, Otis? Does that sound like a deal?"

"That'll be a deal," said Otis, half-heartedly.

Otis was a shy boy with great, round glasses, which he had gotten for his eleventh birthday and which would slide down his nose whenever he looked at his feet (which was most of the time). He would always bury himself in a book and pour over some new word or idea. His parents hectored him to go outside. More often than not, they would find him reading on his bed, snoozing at his little desk, or sticking his tongue out the corner of his mouth while he practiced his cursive.

History and handwriting were his favorite subjects in school, and his teacher, Miss Georgina, a recent graduate from the McElvain School for Teachers, *class of '49*, said that he was very bright and always eager to do his reading. Otis knew that Dad had not really understood why his own son did not like going outdoors and playing with the other children, so, on the weekends, Dad sent him to his grandparents' house, out beyond the town limits. "It'll help the boy get used to the outside. It did wonders for me when I was his age, and I don't see a reason why it shouldn't work for him."

When Otis's father told Grandpa all this, the old man had simply nodded his hoary head and taken a sip from his iced tea. Mimi had glared over the counter at the back of her son's head, almost losing a finger in the carrots she was chopping. After Otis's parents had deposited him on the porch, they gave him a final hug, kiss, and a wave, then sped off down the country road.

Grandpa had come up beside him and put a hand on his shoulder.

"Can I ask you something, sport?"

"Sure," said Otis, looking down, his glasses slipping forward. His parents had not allowed him to take his *Tom Sawyer* with him because he shouldn't have to think about reading over at Grandpa and Mimi's.

"Have you ever seen the Encyclopedia Britannica?" asked Grandpa, watching a drifting cloud.

Otis looked up for what must have been the first time that day. "You have a copy of it?"

"Volumes actually," said Grandpa. He took another sip of his iced tea.

"We've only got two at home. A through B. Pretty old now, too."

"Well... how does thirty brand-spankin'-new volumes sound to you?" said Grandpa, smiling at his grandson. "They're upstairs in the library. We also got a copy of *Treasure Island* for your perusal if you so desire. I hafta catch up on today's news, so if you go on up, I'll join you with a plate of Mimi's cookies and the paper. How does that sound?"

"That'll be a deal!"

"*That'll be a deal?*" repeated Grandpa through a grin.

"Yeah, you know," said Otis. "It means... yeah! Or, sure thing, you know?"

"I like that," said Grandpa, nodding to himself. "That'll be a deal."

On that day, Otis fell in love with Mimi and Grandpa's house. He'd always ask his parents when he could go back. He'd check the calendar and count down the days until he would be dropped off on their porch, suitcase in hand. He'd even grown to love fishing, an activity he used to loathe because of the smell and the sliminess of the fish that would get on his hands. Now he wanted to go fishing at least once during his weekend stays, mainly because Grandpa would tell him stories about the pirate

Blackbeard. He might even tell a few tales about his time in the army, which Otis could never quite tell were real or not. In Otis's mind, they were almost always true.

That weekend, Grandpa had a meeting. He had been working on his car all morning to get the machine *road ready*, as he called it. Like a nurse in an operating room, Otis passed the tools into his grandpa's wise, old hands and wiped his fingers when Grandpa did, even though his hands were never covered in grease.

Now Otis sat on the steps of his grandparents' porch, glaring at the wheels of the car while Grandpa clapped the hood of the old blue Ford shut. He looked over at Otis and then back at his car, scratching his head. He was balding, though he denied it, his hair nearly as white and downy as chicken feathers.

Grandpa came over to Otis and stood in front of the steps with hands in his pockets, chewing his lip. He took out a handkerchief from his overalls and wiped his brow. All about them, there was a smell of freshly cut grass mixed with oil and sun-dried denim streaked with sweat. Otis looked up at him expectantly, pushing his glasses back up and watching the white caterpillar eyebrows pull themselves together in thought.

"What I said still stands, Otis," said Grandpa, at last. "Sorry, buddy." He walked on by and patted Otis's head. "Why don't you go and get some of those crawlers out of Mimi's garden ready up for fishin', hmm?"

Grandpa banged the screen door shut and then the front door behind that. Otis heard the muffled sounds of voices, old married people's voices, comfortable and calm. *Mom and Dad talk that way sometimes,* Otis thought to himself, *but not all the time. They're a lot louder at home.*

He watched Grandpa's car sitting there in the front drive. The blue of the paint glowed in the morning light like the car was brand new, just rolled off the showroom at Treat's Automotive back in town, though it was several years old. Grandpa made a point to polish the bumpers and hubcaps every weekend. It was a roomy thing, full of hot, leathery-smelling air with huge, long seats front and back.

A warm, June-bug quiet hung over the property. Otis contemplated the car with its shiny metal cab, the air shimmering with heat. He thought of the space behind the front seats and how Grandpa had hidden Otis's old rocking horse there, covering it with a quilt.

Otis looked behind him. There was no movement that he could see beyond the lace curtain of the kitchen window. He patted his pockets and felt the clack of the three skipping stones that he had found that morning by the porch and heard the chink of pennies. Twelve cents worth, which was a lot by his estimation. He pushed his glasses up again to the bridge of his nose, taking one last look around him, and saw no one.

With his heart in his mouth, Otis ducked under the window and dashed across the front drive to the back door of the car. The space behind the driver's seat swallowed him, and he pressed his shoulders against the leather. He found the quilt folded on the back seat and pulled it over himself. He did everything he could to make himself smaller and smaller. Then he heard Grandpa raise his voice.

"Otis? Otis!"

He did not move. Beads of sweat rolled down his cheeks, but he kept still.

"Otis!"

Come on, Otis thought to himself. *Please, please, just get in the car and go to Hanesey's. It's so hot already!* Otis swore he could feel himself begin to cook. He heard the door open and felt pressure against his shoulders as Grandpa sank into his seat with the sigh that only old men knew how to make. The car rumbled to life and, with a powerful motion, rolled out of the drive. It dropped onto the street that passed by the property and moved on into town.

The ride was short, though it was full of bumps and turns. Otis braced himself for a sudden stop and made sure that he did not jostle against the back of Grandpa's seat. For the entire ride, he did his best to hold his breath almost all the way to *Hanesey's*.

Soon enough, the car came to a stop outside of the store, purring in the shade of the butternut tree that grew there. Grandpa turned the key in the ignition and let the engine die.

"Well gah-lee," said Grandpa to himself with a sigh. "This back'll kill me one day. Wha' ever happened to aging gracefully?"

Otis heard the clack of the door action and felt the shift of weight when Grandpa got out of his seat. After a second, Otis peeked from under the quilt and, inching upward, peered out the window to see Grandpa standing there in his clean shirt, slacks, and suspenders, rubbing the small of his back. Otis ducked down again and waited until he heard the door close. There was a moment where Otis thought Grandpa might come back. Then Otis heard the click of the lock and the shuffle of steps up the sidewalk.

Otis slid up his hand and popped the handle of the door. *Hanesey's Drugstore* had a glass front and windows that wrapped around the sides so that the clerks who were working the front could see anybody coming up Mainstreet. Otis had to be particularly careful. He poked his head over the back of the driver's seat to try and get a fix on Grandpa.

There he was, strolling down the sidewalk to a table that sat under the shade of the awning, in the company of four graywood rocking chairs. Two old men were already there, bottles of root-beer sweating on the table between them. They stood up with a laugh that Otis heard through the blue tinted glass of the car. As carefully as he could, he slid out onto the pavement and then push the door, until he heard it shut. The three old men talked while he slid around the back of the car.

"Well golly gee, Isaac. It's good to see you again!"

"Sure, sure, Willie, and how's the wife treatin' ya?"

"Fine, you old man, just dandy! The grandkids come down once a month from Chicago, and it's real nice to have some company besides the bride every once in a while, but my, my, it's exhausting having all those rapscallions running around your feet! How about yourself, old man? Grandkid doing alright?"

"Otis? Oh, he's fine. In fact, he's in—"

"Naw, tell us about 'im later, old man," said the other one of Grandpa's friends, who had been quiet up until that point. "Are we gonna play a game of poker, or what?"

"'Course we are, what do you think I am, a flat? Come on now, get the cards. You gotta drink set for me? Fine, fine..."

Otis crept out from behind the car and dashed to the side door of *Hanesey's* where "EMPLOYEES ONLY" was stenciled on the glass. He opened the door.

"Sorry, Mr. Hanesey!" Otis blurted.

"What in blue blazes are you doing here?!" Mr. Hanesey sat up from his desk, squinting at the boy that had just appeared out of nowhere.

"I'm real sorry, Mr. Hanesey! I had to get on through your store and—"

"Then use the front door like a civilized person might, you young rogue. Now get out of my office before I tan your hide!" The words were not as harsh as he might have expected, but still they had a sharpness to them that left no room for interpretation. Otis scampered through the door that led to that wonderfully clean smell of talc, French soap, and newly polished tile. A clerk was behind the counter.

"And what'll ya have, Master Otis?"

"How much'll this get me, Mr. Rane?" Otis looked around the store to make sure he was alone while he fished in his pocket. He set down a scatter of pennies on the high countertop and then shoved them into a tiny miserly pile. The clerk looked down at the collection of coins, squinting, and seemed to run a calculation in his head before he nodded.

"That'll get ya a Payday, Master Otis!" the clerk declared.

"Shhh, Mr. Rane!" Otis shot a glance over his shoulder toward the door. "I don't want them to find me out!"

"Find ya out? Whatchu hidin' for anyway? Didn't you come here with your Granpapi? I saw you getting' outa that car o' his."

"Yeah, but he doesn't know it!" hissed Otis. He took the candy bar and tucked it safe away into his pocket.

"Don't know it?" chuckled Mr. Rane, shaking his head. "You mean you sneaked into the back o' his car without 'im findin' out? Shaw, child, you don' think yo Grandpapi is that dumb, do ya?"

"He's not dumb," said Otis. "I just snuck by him is all. Now I gotta be quiet, Mr. Rane, or else he'll find me out."

"Mm-hmm. Sure thing," said the clerk, disbelieving. The register let out a musical clang. "Go run on now, and don't mess up that floor! I just mopped it clean, and I won't have all your tracks goin' around and muckin' it up!"

"Yes sir, Mr. Rane."

"Mm-hmm." He turned his back on Otis with the air of a man that had much better things to do.

"Uh, Mr. Rane, you think it be okay if I sit out there?" asked Otis and pointed through the glass to a seat that was behind the corner where the three men sat. Grandpa and the other two had their backs turned to the side window and were looking out across the street, so they could not see the seats that were behind them.

"Mm-hmm," Mr. Rane said again. He busied himself with the contents of the shelves behind the register.

"Can I use a side door?"

"Now what's the matter witchu? Can't use the front door like a normal boy? Too good fo' it?"

"No sir, I just want to stay secret is all. Please? Please can I use the side door?"

"Fine... through there. Don't touch nothin', understand?"

"Yessir! I won't touch a thing, sir!"

"Bettah not, or else I'll tattle for sure."

"Yessir, Mr. Rane."

No Truce With The Furies

Otis went through the back room where unopened boxes of candy and crates of soda were piled all the way to the ceiling.

He opened the rusty door that led to an alley at the back of the store, before stepping out, then slowly closing it again. As he made his way around the back of the store, he snickered to himself. *I'm a master sleuth, no doubt of it.* Now he could sit just off to the side and out of sight, around the corner, so that they wouldn't discover him. Settling himself, he realized that he hadn't really thought about what he was going to do. He just wanted to listen to what the old men talked about.

He sat down in an oversized rocking chair with his back to the street and began to unwrap the candy bar quietly so the tearing paper wouldn't disturb the old men.

With his back turned, Otis missed the winks exchanged by the old men while they shuffled the deck, cut, and dealt according to the rule of play. Grandpa hooked a thumb over his shoulder, and the one named Willie nodded, before putting two pennies in the pot.

"Hold Me Darlin's the game, gentlemen, with two to play for the Big Blind," said Willie. He looked at his cards.

"Well shucks," said the other, who folded out of turn. "I tell you something, Willie, you always dealt terrible cards."

"Miserable," sighed Grandpa, who was the Little Blind. He put the rest of his ante in.

"But I'm still your huckleberry."

"Yes sirree!" said Willie, laying out the Flop. "Been that way since the *war*."

"Sure, sure." Grandpa nodded. "And what exactly was it you did during the war, Willie? Push pencils? Check forms?"

"That's what you would think, old timer," laughed Willie. "When all you did was polish some general's boots."

"Some general?" said Grandpa incredulously. "Listen here, you whippersnapper. That was not some general, by golly! It was the commander-in-chief of the army, and I won't have you go around and say he was just another officer or what-have-you."

"But you did shine his boots," said the other old timer, taking a sip of his root beer.

"Sure, I did!" The Turn was dealt, and Grandpa scowled at his cards. "I was also with him at that big battle. You remember the one... *Whoever dealt these cards deals crap*..." Grandpa put in his bet. "I'm in."

"Shiloh? Vicksburg?" asked Willie.

"Vicksburg! That's the one! It's been so long."

"How many years now?" asked the other old man.

"Oh, don't remind me," said Grandpa, shaking his head. "Every time I look at the calendar, it brings to mind exactly how old I am, and, frankly, my wife does enough of that for me. *'You know,'* she says to me, all precious like, *'you're not gettin' any younger, and neither am I. Sooner or later, we'll be so bent over with age that we'll be touchin' our toes!'* Now how's that for a reminder, eh?" They all laughed, and the cards were dealt.

Otis frowned at his Payday. He knew his Grandpa was in the army, but how long ago was that? He had gone to France, fought the Germans, and come back. What was it?, forty years ago? Vicksburg sounded German alright, but the name Shiloh kept nagging at the back of his mind, trying to pry loose a memory he had from school. He chewed on his candy while the old men finished their hand and started another.

"How could you forget Vicksburg, Isaac?" asked Willie, putting in his ante. "I remember it clear as day. I never forgot that advance we made up that hill with its fortifications, them da—I mean—dad-gum rebs holdin' up the place."

"Well, well," said Grandpa magnanimously, by which it was obvious that he had a good hand. "Do you remember the shovels when we tried to redirect the river? The whole Mississippi like we were all Hercules. Hmph! Do you remember having to burn our uniforms because there were so many fleas? Every night the bonfires rising up, and you could hear the fleas goin' *pop, pop, pop!* Boy, we were miserable."

Otis chewed hesitantly. *The Mississippi wasn't in Germany*, he thought.

"But d'ya remember that little aide de camp?" asked the other old man, folding once more. "You know the one. What was his name? Private... Private..."

"Private Pitts! That was the man!" laughed Grandpa. "What an unfortunate last name."

"Right! Remember how he used to get so drunk that he would holler out in the middle of the night, wake up half the camp?"

"Oh, do I!"

"Right?" said the other old man. "And do you remember that one mornin', when Pitts was supposed to be goin' out with us and the General to inspect the line, but he was a no show? Gone off, I thought, with some local girl, but no such luck 'cause then we wouldn'a had to clean up after his mess. So, I'm gettin' everything ready, and you're there, Isaac, fixin' up the General's horse. Then, all of a sudden, this bugle boy comes in, all huffin' and puffin', sayin' we gotta come see what Pitts's done. So, we follow the bugle boy, and what do we find? What do we find but Pitts at the edge of the camp, naked as the day he was born and sittin' on a colonel's horse backward, singin' some darn fool thing or other about how he always wanted to be in the cavalry. Boy, he never lived that down, Pitts did. In fact, when we marched into the city on the fourth, our company sang that song 'Yankee Doodle,' but with a line that said that he rode into town, *naked* on a pony!"

"What a character," laughed Grandpa. "And I tell you, Pitts may be a poor example of a soldier, but, my friends, I must tell you that the secret to as long a life as we have now is nothin' short of a responsible consumption of *liquor*. That's all! I don't care what the temperance ladies claim. They don't know their heads from their tails or their right from their left about liquor. I tell you, the only reason I look as good as I do know is because of that flask I have under my pillow at home."

"A regular bonafide *Methuselah*," said Willie. "You don't look a day over ninety-three."

Otis's candy bar dropped into his lap. Now he remembered. He had learned about the battle of Vicksburg in school, reading about how the Union captured it on Independence Day, 1863. *But that was impossible,* he thought. He looked down at his fingers as he calculated the years, counting by tens and then fives and then by singles. He counted again and again, double and triple checking his estimations. *If Grandpa had been sixteen when he went to war...*

Otis leapt from his seat, not caring about the candy he left on the porch, and ran around the corner where he stood before the three men, open mouthed in disbelief.

"You're over *a hundred* years old!" he exclaimed. Grandpa froze, his root beer between the table and his open mouth. The other men at the table put down their cards and drinks to watch.

"Otis!" Grandpa said, standing up out of his rocking chair. "Where on earth did you come from?"

"No, Grandpa! You don't understand!"

"I don't?"

"You're old! You are really, *really* old! How are you alive, Grandpa! I thought you were only in one war! I think you set a record, Grandpa, I really do. There's no way that you didn't. We have to check the record. Is there a record book out there we can check?"

"You're not going to let go of this, are ya?"

"You're old, Grandpa! Not just a little bit old but a *lot* old!"

The other men were bent over their cards from the force of their laughter, wiping away tears.

⚜   ⚜   ⚜

Later on, Grandpa and Otis stood at the front counter of *Hanesey's* while Mr. Rane was bagging a prescription for Grandpa in a white paper sack. Otis couldn't stop staring up at his Grandpa, unable to get past the revelation of the past few minutes. Grandpa, of course, was as cool as cool could be. In fact, he seemed to be enjoying his grandson's company far more than would have been expected. His friends had laughed off the boy's sudden disruption of their game, finished a round, and offered Otis a sip of their root beers. But Otis couldn't accept the proffered drinks, as he was too jittery by half, bobbing from one foot to the other, not sure what to do next.

Mr. Rane handed Grandpa his bag with the prescription, and Grandpa passed him the money that rustled like green butterflies. Mr. Rane shook his head at Otis, then eyed Grandpa.

"I think there's a screw loose in tha' one, sir," he said. "Got all excited over a number."

"It's not just a number, Mr. Rane!" exclaimed Otis. "It's a *really* big number! He's over a hundred—"

"Alright now," Grandpa interrupted, taking the bag and shaking Mr. Rane's hand.

"'Course, sir. Anytime."

He looked at Otis, who was pacing back and forth and looking down, then back up, having to constantly push his glasses up the bridge of his nose.

"Since you decided to bomb the party, I don't see why we can't go fishin' now, 'cept this time Willie and Tom will be joining us."

"*Really?*" asked Otis, not quite believing what Grandpa had said.

"Yep. Since you busted up our card game, I'm bringin' them along. Willie's a good fisherman, and Tom's not half bad, so we'll do alright. But listen here!" he said sternly, finger raised with near imperial authority. "You are goin' to be *quiet*. You are goin' to be *respectful*. And, most important of all, you will not ask so many questions that our ears fall off. Do you understand?"

Otis stood, stock-still, eyes wide open. He had rarely heard Grandpa be this strict. Otis nodded.

"That'll be a deal," he said, gravely.

Grandpa pursed his lips. "Good," he said. "Now let's get in the car, and, before you ask, no, we are not goin' by the library."

They had to drive back to the house first to get their poles and tackle. Willie and Tom said they would meet them with their own gear at a place where the fish were known to bite. It was all a big joke to them and a welcome, if unexpected, addition to their day. Otis was quiet on the drive to the house and snatched quick, secretive glimpses of his Grandpa, who kept his eyes on the road, driving like nothing had changed.

"Grandpa?"

"Yep?"

"What's in the white bag?"

"Medicine for my back," he said. "You get this old, you need some medicine to keep you goin'. It's like motor oil but for old people."

"What about the flask?"

"You heard that, too, huh?" mused Grandpa with a grin. "Yeah, well... Don't go tellin' that to your Mom or Dad. They wouldn't like it too much. I wouldn't mention it to Mimi, now that I think of it. Don't tell anyone, in fact. We'll just keep that our secret. How does that sound?"

"Yessir."

"Okay then, here we are," said Grandpa, rolling the car into the drive. "Go on in, and get your tackle. I'll get mine."

"Yessir!" Otis ran.

Mimi stood up in her front garden, hands on her hips, and watched him rush into the house from the shade of her sunhat. *"Wipe your feet!"* she called out, but it was too late. The screen door slapped behind him with a rush of summer air. Grandpa left the motor running and walked over to his wife, shoes kicking at the gravel of the drive. She raised an eyebrow in that way that she had. He leaned over and gave her a kiss on the cheek.

"Back so soon?" she asked. "And I thought Otis wasn't coming along with you to the store."

"I thought that, too," sighed Grandpa. "But the rascal hitched a ride-along anyway. I thought I saw him. Me and the boys talked about *Vicksburg*."

"Oh, *that* story? Isaac! You know better!"

Grandpa laughed and scratched the back of his head. "Yeah, well... I just couldn't resist. He was right there, and I just felt like..."

"That you couldn't resist and had to tell somebody, right?"

"Yep, sorry."

"That poor boy is going to think that you and I are just a bunch of honest-to-goodness fossils now, isn't he? How old now, a hundred? Two hundred? Really Isaac, that's just silly."

Grandpa chuckled to himself. "Not only that... but I mentioned the flask, too."

"The flask? Oh, my Lord, Isaac..."

Noah W. Newmann

No Truce With The Furies

Pickett's Field

RAIN FALLS *PITTER-PAT* in the dust. The stone porch stretches out beneath me, polished by years of life. It reminds me of Ma's porch when I was young. That was a decade ago. I went to school for medicine in the years between. Now I am dressed in modern fashion: black hat, coat, and shoes, buckled, cinched, and crammed on—the perfect picture of a doctor. Ma is gone now, my sister eloped, and my brother tends the family farm. I am alone. Now holding my bag at my side, I wonder how I have gotten to where I stand on the porch under the weeping eaves of a country home, a pistol to my head.

A steel-lipped kiss is all I am, a point of simple and terrible being while the water from the eaves taps on my shoulders. The man's eyes are owlishly wide. His breath is heavy and drawn out, stretched thin. The air is run with a stale carpet of whiskey, an old haunt from school. It smells of late-night cabarets and wet soaked alleys.

The moment is all I feel. The rain is still, hanging feverishly. The man is hunched, eyes bloodshot, pupils wide as pits. But his hand is steady, and he watches with a keen interest. We each take the other's breath like thieves.

"Wha' d'ya want, eh?"

My glasses, beaded with rainwater, slide down my nose.

"I... came from town."

"Who sen' ya?"

"My secretary—I have a secretary. She brought me the call and said it was urgent, so... I came as soon as I could."

"Bastard."

"What?"

"Tha' bastard boy! She tol' th' boy, didin' she? Didn' she? Sen' th' boy ou' to tell ya, eh?" The barrel presses. He shakes his head like he has just rolled in sand, all the while keeping that gun fixed dead on my temple. It is a point in space, absolute.

"Yer a policema', ain't ya? Come t' my 'ouse to pull me away, eh? Well, ye ain't gettin' me this time, ya sonofa—"

"Sir, I am a doctor!"

"A wha'?"

"I'm a doctor, on a house call. I'm not a policeman." My glasses are so low now that there is a danger they might fall off. The man's head cocks to the side, and he scratches under his hat.

"Doctor, eh? Tha's true? Really?"

"Yes."

"Well... if tha's th' case..." The gun lowers slowly, roving over a brow. It knocks against my nose, catching my glasses. The barrel pulls the frames until they fall, and I blink, trying, failing to pull away the haze. The man's face is a blur with no distinctive features, a silhouette in the light that shines through the doorway. I reach down to where I heard the glasses tumble, but a call stops me.

"Woah, now... Where d'ya think yer goin'?"

"I need my glasses," I say, hand pawing at the stone. "I can't see without them."

"Sure ya can," said Mr. Pickett. "I know ya *in-tel-lec-tual* types. Ya just wear 'em to make yerself look th' part. Do I got tha' right? Jus' pick 'em up."

I scramble for them, grasp them, and stand up straight. I put them on, and look into his face, saying nothing.

"Well? Come in! If'n ya wanna stay ou' with the cayoots, I'll let ya! I don' wan' yer type in 'ere, bu' if th' woman wan's it, she'll ge' wha's comin'..." He waves me through the door, and I step through, dazed, hand out. Mr. Pickett bats it away, and lumbers ahead, carrying that smell of liquor along with him.

"Where is Mrs. Pickett?"

"Through 'ere."

He points, and I follow.

Someone had telephoned my office while I was out on another call. My secretary handed me the note before I even had the chance to sit myself down. All the while, she complained about that new telephone I had purchased and how everyone was listening in on the line. The call had come from the old telegraph station where a boy said that a Mrs. Pickett on her family's farm was hurt something fierce and needed the doctor's help right away.

The door creaks open, and gloom leaks out with the smell of stale sweat and soiled sheets. There is a window that rattles with rain and a lit candle on the side table.

"Over 'ere." I see the metal of the gun shine like a wand in the dim. "She been sick all o' three days. No good... Nobody t' wash or do th' kiddies' own sup..." The gun drops, and heavy steps fill the door, leaving me to my work. I set down my bag and roll up my sleeves, squinting at the shadows that make up the room. I feel for her neck, then find the artery and its beat. It is weak. Sweat lacquers her skin, and her breathing is shallow.

"Mrs. Pickett, are you awake? Can you hear me?" Her head turns, and a hand stirs beneath the sheets. The linen shifts like beach sand. "Mrs. Pickett? Can you tell me your Christian name?"

"Martha..." comes the answer.

"Martha?"

"Yeah, Martha! Martha's 'er name!" Mr. Pickett's voice crashes like a stone through a window. I ignore it.

"Martha. My name is Herrn, and I'm a doctor. I'm here to check up on you, to see if I can help, alright?"

She pants, trying to sit up. "...Doctor Herrn?"

"Yes. I'm here to look after you. Easy now."

"But I... know you. Don't you... recognize me?

I look up from my bag. While I watch, the face comes up to me through the gloom, her nose and hair clear. All at once, like an epiphany, I see her as plainly as a man in heaven sees God. I knew her and knew her very well.

When I used to play with the boys from across town, they would make fun of me for my weak eyes, snatch the glasses from my nose, parade around, turning them upside down, and mocking me. Watching from the steps of Ma's house, she would stand, herself, Ma in miniature, ball her fists and step between us. She was the friend whom I thought I had lost when I was away at school for all those years. She had eloped without a word and was never seen again. There had not even been a letter. Now, she was sweating under yellowed sheets, my sister.

"Martha..." What was the right thing for me to say? Looking for answers to this is worse than looking for a knife in a crowded drawer—and then there was that shadow behind me. I could say nothing for myself. Like a parrot, I mimic my old teachers and ask my sister, *my patient,* the necessary questions.

"Do you have any aching or sharp pain? Any discomfort in the abdomen?"

"Abdo—what?"

"Your belly, Martha. Do you have any sharp pains, or is it a dull ache?"

"No. But I do have an ache in my back... and sometimes it flares up..."

I reach under her, probing with my fingers. She grunts when I lift the blouse. The skin is patchy and discolored across her ribs, like a stain. I take the candle from the bedside, holding it so I can get a better look at the bruise. It is circular and red as a plumb. I urge Martha to turn over, and, when she does, I see another spread over the small of the back.

"Hey. Hey, wha' ya doin' to 'er, eh?"

"I am examining my patient, Mr. Pickett. Here, hold the light."

"No, ya ain't lookin' a' 'er like tha'! Tha' ain't righ'!"

"Pay no... attention to him," Martha says. "He's all bark... No bite." The smile is strained. The words exhaust her.

"Martha? Has he..." I look for better words to say. "Have you had a... *fall* lately?" I lean close and see her nod. "Have you had any sickness? Vomiting?"

"Wait..." says Pickett, thrusting his head forward. He scratched under his hat. "Sugar? Ya know th' doc?"

"I do... He's that brother I told you about... Went to school six years back? 'Fore I met you."

I hear heavy, booted feet draw close. While I set down the candle and replace the blouse, Martha's hand reaches out and grabs mine. It is not like it used to be. It has been replaced by tissue paper.

"Have you seen the children? The little girl and my boy? Near grown now, almost as handsome as their paw."

"He ain't grown yet," said Pickett, swaying by the table. "Let go o' 'im, Sugar."

"Have you had any vomiting, Martha?" Again, she nods. Her eyes glance to Pickett's gun, which shines bright in the candlelight.

I open my bag with one hand and hold onto hers with another. "Sir," I say, in as even a tone as I can manage. "I believe your wife has an infection of the kidney. It is caused, in this case, by a severe blow to the lower back, and if it goes untreated, there might be some serious repercussions. I am prescribing—"

"Caused by a wha'?"

"A blow administered by a blunt object." I stand and pull Martha's fingers from mine. "It can be caused by a very bad fall or the administration of a cane or stick that is blunt, to the back and sides where the kidneys are."

"Wha'? Ya mean like a whippin'?"

"Something like that." I sort and draw out a bottle from my bag, corked, labeled, and I set it on the table beside the light. "I am prescribing this to take after every meal. One spoonful, three times a day, until the bottle is finished. No strenuous activity, no lifting of heavy loads, and make sure she gets plenty of light and air."

Pickett holds up the bottle in front of the candle and watches the medicine turn lazily between his fingers. I close my bag. My hands are shaking.

"I will come back in three days to check up on her, to make sure that she is recovering well."

"How much will it cos' me?"

"There's no charge."

"How much, I said!" His eyes are wide, like saucers. His words are clear and clipped. "There's always a price with yer kind, ain't there? Ain't there!"

"Sugar, don't yell, please..."

"SHUT UP, WOMAN!"

I cannot see it all, though I see enough to know what happens next. His hand, which holds the bottle, swings to throw it at me. The bottle flies out, and I see it arc to the window where it shatters into a thousand droplets of light. The shards fall over my sister, and she is crying, hands over her face. I turn away from her, bag in hand. Pickett's face flushes and sweats fury over parted lips and he weeps, staggering away from me, off balance.

"I'm sorry, I'm sorry, I'm sorry. I didn't mean to. I'm sorry. Oh God, please, I'm sorry..." He says those words like a spell, as if they had some power to undo what he had done.

I remember myself, and my hand snaps out, clutches his collar. It is like he has left all his weight in his clothes, and there is nothing of him but the mumbling of words. I pull him with me.

There are two children in the kitchen, who watch us go by, their faces like little moons peeking out from behind the rough-wood table, pale while I pull their father through the door that was left open.

There is a fence at the edge of a muddy field, and I let him go, leave him clinging to the white-painted post. I take the gun from him, and, for a moment, consider the shining weapon, its stock sleek with rain, but then I hurl it out, and it flies, until it falls like a star into the sopping field. He is crying still, though the storm drowns it.

The smell that follows me back into the house is that of rain and mud. Water pools under my boots while I tell the children to gather their things. The little moons vanish with a pitter-patter of feet.

With a handkerchief, I dab at Martha's face to free it of the medicine that has spilled over her. After a struggle and a tinkle of glass, I lift her out of the bed while thunder rolls over the clouds.

We leave.

I place her in the back of my buggy with the youngest child. I drape a blanket over them to shield them from the rain, but the water drips through, like a weeping cloud. The oldest, a boy of five, straw hat pulled over his dark eyebrows, points my way down the road. At one point, he takes the reins of the horse and pulls. I hear the stones trickle over themselves when the wheels stop.

"What's wrong?" I ask and stare ahead, blind from the rain on my glasses. "Have I steered us wrong?" There is a crack that makes the horse jump, though there is no flash of lighting.

"It's nothin'." He hands the reins back to me, and I give them a gentle flick. The horse knows its way to town. The boy curls against me. His hat nearly falls off when I put my arm around his shoulder.

"Paw's lying in the field is all," he says.

Over

"WE ALL HAVE TO die sometime," I say, pulling my gloves tight. My brother looks at me, mute. He pulls on his pipe—The smoke is as gray as his wrinkled, dirty uniform. I take up my rifle and lay myself against the boards and bags of sand that make the walls of our trench. The walls are a kind of binder for the earth. More smoke puffs from hand-rolled cigarettes and crooked mouths, stinking. I am drowning in the thick, fuggy air while I put on my gas mask.

Artillery cracks a mile behind the mud and craters filled with bloody water, the heads of horses half in, half out. It is what is left of the Sixth Cavalry. *Will that be me?* Over the pockmarked field, there is a poisoned haze, the color of plague. The haze is ours, and the wind—for now—is with us, holding the gas by the corners like some devil's rug.

"Bayonette raparieren!"

I feel the lines stir at the words of the commandant. I feel the men behind me moving their rifles. I feel their nervousness when they fix bayonets. We are warriors, spears shining in the summer sun. I hear another round of artillery, the whistle of shells coming to grind us all to dust. My brother is smoking. His mask is hanging under his chin like a second head, staring, wide-eyed, anticipating. *When will the shell hit? In five seconds or three? Two? I was always good with numbers—*

An explosion.

The dugout erupts to my left. Something spatters on my helmet. Something clatters on my canteen: a soldier stumbling into me. Someone is screaming. Everything is blurred. I cannot understand.

It is the commandant screaming. He grabs a man who is sobbing and throws him back to the wall of the trench, telling him to gird himself, *be a man*. My heart thunders in double time while our own good men return the shells in battery. I think of us all, lined like matches in a box, waiting for our heads to be struck—caught by sniper fire. *My God...* There is a break in the yellow fog, and the air hisses before something makes the turf geyser near my brother's head. He ducks down, pawing the soil from his eye. He sobs as he fixes his mask, eyes shut behind round glass. Another man is not so lucky, and I hear the metal of a helmet shear.

We are not brave. We are not warriors. We are boys from a city where old men sit safely in their cafés and tell stories. A lie is a story. *My God... Did I send Elena her letter? Of course I did. Folded just right; I was always good with numbers, measurements. One fold here, another here, and then across and again to seal the words dated '18. I know I handed it to the messenger boy, ragged, thin as a picket.* I pull from my pocket the photograph, dirt falling down from the top of the trench and tapping her face, her eyes, and over her white dress... *My God.*

"Dreissig Sekunden... Alles beriet auf meinem Zeichen!"

Only the moment, only the feeling. Boots grind cigarettes into the duckboard. My brother, hands shaking, flicks out the tobacco from his pipe and buttons the pipe into his pocket. If he goes, it is mine. He promised me so long ago. *What? An hour? A week?* I feel the seconds crash through, every move of the hand a cannonade. *My God!* I tuck the photo into my pocket, close it tight. *Will I see her again? My God...*

"Jedes Soldat erfüllt seine Pflicht. Fünfzehn Sekunden!"

What is he saying? My throat is dry... *My God.*

Hot breath on my neck. My goggles fog and blind me. *My God!*

"Und Alles... über!"

My God, my God, my God—MY GOD!

The whistle of the commandant, tiny, shrieking under the roar of the cannon fire, throws us from the belly of the trench. Up and over, we run.

We stumble through the yellow curtain of cloud to the enemy line.

We are boys, and we are warriors—a tide of thousands.

Revelations

I ONCE MET A MAN on the train to Istanbul. When I found the man, he was in a railcar suite where the seats face one another. He held his head in his hands, suitcase between his knees. In need of some company, I took the opposite seat.

"Good afternoon," I said and sidled in, which clattered my luggage against the glass door. There came no reply from the man.

"Say... are you alright?" I asked. I hoisted my suitcase onto the luggage rack above my seat.

"Yes... yes," came the answer. "I'm fine."

I took off my hat and hung it on the hook and slid the clouded glass door shut. I set my briefcase down and then sat. Fishing in my pockets for a pack of cigarettes gave me a chance to get a look at my new neighbor. He was dressed like me: a fashionable three-piece suit, black wool pinstripes with black polished shoes to match. His collar was starched stiff as a board, with a tie that was knotted so tight you would have thought it would choke the life out of an ordinary man. Simply looking at the knot made me want to adjust my own, to loosen the silk that now felt like a hangman's noose.

I finally got my last pack of French-made cigarettes out from my coat pocket and felt its weight. "*Dammit*," I muttered, half to myself and half to my neighbor.

I had not had a good smoke in about a day. Between all the meetings, the stops, and the rushings from place to place, I had only enough time to check my daybook. My nerves were frayed and fragile, and my hands were shaking (something that never recommended a businessman).

I patted my other pockets, even though I knew I would not find anything there. The train lurched forward with a mechanized *hiss,* and the platform outside the window of our compartment began to slide on past. An idea came to me.

"Say," I asked. "Neighbor, do you happen to have a smoke on you, by any chance? Looks like I've run out." The bellows-like huffing of the locomotive grew louder while the train gathered speed. The man glanced up at me for the first time, one hand over his mouth. He wore a hat I thought was out of order with the rest of him because it was battered, with a wrinkled brim that hung low over his eyes. It gave him the appearance of someone who had just come out of the rain, though the sky outside was clear and blue. He reached up, pinched the brim, and tugged it absentmindedly, giving me a hint of how the thing had come to look that way.

"Here," he mumbled, over the rattle of train cars. He reached and produced a pack from his waistcoat pocket. For a brief second, he considered the pack and then thrust it toward me. "Take it."

He did his best to smile, to pull his lips back to show his teeth. His eyes, however, did not smile. They showed nothing of the man opposite me, simply staring. I took the pack from him, crumpling my empty one before I tossed it toward the wire waste bin that sat in the corner.

"Thank you kindly," I said. I gave the pack a little shake to feel the rattle of cigarettes. There were maybe ten if I had to guess. "So..." I said, opening the pack and giving my neighbor an expectant look. "Do you mind if I smoke here?"

"Go ahead."

"Fine. Fine." I took out a match. "What brand?"

"You've never heard of 'em."

"Try me! You never know. I've smoked them all—or all the good ones. *Damn...*"

"No lucifers on you? Matches, I mean."

"How'd you guess?" I laughed. The man reached out and gave me a matchbook. "Thank you." I tapped out a cigarette, clinched it in my teeth, and, while I got ready to strike the match, I examined the packaging.

The box was red, bright as a fire engine. It was the kind of red that made your eyes smart a bit to see it, the kind that grabbed you by the lapels and said, *here I am!* On the front, there was a picture of gold spectacles with eyes that peered sadly through the delicate rounds. Under the eyes ran a name in white print trimmed with the same gold that made the spectacles: "Revelation Cigarettes."

I wondered at the box and turned it in my hand. My neighbor was right. I had not heard of these. Must have been small manufacturer out of London. I set it down on my knee and squinted at the back of the packaging while I cupped the light to the end of the cigarette.

When it caught, I drew the smoke in deeply and held it there. It leaped down my throat, almost as if it were breathing for me.

The drug began its work. Nicotine shot through me, and my hands steadied.

"Where'd you get these?" I asked through a rush of smoke.

All I heard was a slide and a click when the door latch caught. I looked up. The man was gone, and a shadow passed just outside the cloudy glass. "Well damn me," I said and stood up. I waved the match out before I opened the door.

A few passengers were walking down the corridor: A gentleman stepped aside for two ladies in fashionable dresses, and a porter in a green coat and white gloves was helping with baggage. There was no sign whatsoever of my former companion. I stood there, nonplussed, wondering what I was going to do. I took a drag on the cigarette.

"*He probably jumped*," said a voice. It was on the edge of my hearing.

I turned to see where the voice had come from. The conductor was walking up behind me. He was a portly man in a blue hat with a brass plaque over the brim and a fine set of whiskers. He was smiling and checking the time on his tiny gold watch.

"Your ticket, if you please, sir."

"I beg your pardon?" I asked.

"Your ticket, *if you please, sir.*"

He held out his hand, fingers like Vienna sausages. I produced the slip of paper, which he summarily inspected and clicked with a pair of metal hole punchers that whined and popped with the compression of the spring. He handed me back the ticket with an officious smile.

"Going all the way, are you?" he asked. It sounded as if he had asked that particular question a thousand times before and that he did not particularly care about the answer.

"Yeah... I am. Say..." I slipped the ticket into my pocket absentmindedly.

The conductor consulted his watch again like he had someplace to be. "Yes, sir?"

"You *did* see a man walk out of this compartment, right?" The conductor followed my finger to look at the cabin number. He shook his head.

"*Who does he think you are? Everyone's keeper?*" This time the voice was louder and not at all faint.

"I beg your—" One of the porters shouldered his way in between us, shooting a glare at me.

"Don't know. Don't care. Don't wanna know. Don't wanna care," muttered the porter to himself. He turned off into one of the compartments. Before he did so, he straightened his back, put on a customer pleasing smile, and opened the door. Women's voices greeted him before the door closed. I shut my mouth.

"People come and go, sir," said the conductor. He pocketed his watch. "Probably just needed some fresh air is all." He eyed the cigarette in my hand and the curl of smoke that rose from the paper and tobacco. "Now, if you'll excuse me, sir. Have a pleasant rest of your day." He went on his way, looking into the various compartments to knock on their doors to cry of "Tickets need be shown for transit! Tickets please!" I shook my head and took another drag, which slid down my throat like ice.

Maybe a breath of fresh air will do me good, I thought. The train was moving, and, while I looked down the cramped passageway, I saw the train car shift and people through the glass of the doors settle down in their seats. Going outside seemed a good idea compared to staying inside, which at once seemed cramped and close with the smoke of my cigarette.

When I stepped out onto the observation platform at the back of the train car, I found a woman standing, arms stiff while she held onto the railing. The train was not yet at full speed, as we were still in the limits of the city. She wore a hat that was tied under her chin with a bright silk band. She did not notice me at first but instead looked out while the buildings sped by, smokestacks and brick façades, shopfronts and avenues.

"Good afternoon," I said, raising my voice over the noise, even though we were practically shoulder to shoulder.

"Good afternoon," she said, startled. A warehouse swooped by. I shielded my cigarette from the gust of wind, knocked off ash on the railing, and took another drag. Her hand was at her throat. She had on white gloves that were very dainty and most likely fitted. She came from money.

"*God, don't you wish you could just... jump?*"

I blinked at the woman, not exactly sure of what I had just heard. I did not say anything. Sometimes it is best to keep quiet when people say things like that.

"Don't you wish that you could just jump? Do you ever have those thoughts?" She smiled at me, as if she had just noticed me. Then, all of a sudden, she shook her head. "I mean, I'm not insane, am I?" she asked. "For having those kinds of thoughts? They just sort of come over me out of nowhere, I guess."

"No. No, no, I understand. You're not the only one who has those thoughts, I think." I smiled at her reassuringly. "I read in a magazine that there's a study of people's brains, where having those kinds of thoughts is not too uncommon. In fact, it's rather pedestrian if those psychologists have it right." She looked relieved.

"*See? You're not the only one who thinks those things.*" Her mouth had not moved, yet I had heard the words as clear as could be.

"Thank God," she said and put a hand on her bonnet to hold it steady in the buffeting wind.

"*You see? He's put-together, and he thinks it's not out of the ordinary. That means you're put-together. In fact, he thinks it's rather pedestrian, if you can believe him. Listen to what he has to say. Ask him where he comes from.*" The voice was sibilant and very much like the woman's. It had a cool, cutting sound to it, and it whispered directly into my ear.

"Is this city home for you?" asked the woman.

"N... no," I stuttered, spooked by the duality of voices. My cigarette's ash came loose again, caught away by the wind. I cupped the light absentmindedly, and, just then, the ember flared. I jerked it closer and sheltered it more from the wind, and there it was again: The glow dimmed and blazed over again, as if it were breathing.

Without thinking, I put it to my lips, and that previous feeling returned with familiarity. The smoke had been cold and brought a very strange sensation along with it, like the smoke itself was sharp. I could feel it then, going over my tongue and hanging at the back of my throat.

Ever since that man had given me the package of cigarettes, ever since the first breath, I had been feeling these things.

Was this cigarette part of some trick? Some illusion? What I had heard—was that part of the same trick? An illusion so powerful that it seemed like magic. But I was a man of science. I no longer believed in magic or mediums or powers beyond one's own control. Other people believed in those kinds of things, but they were charlatans who took advantage of the indolent and the stupid. They were crooks or, worse, they were loons.

I contemplated the breathing ember, collecting my thoughts. Was I going loony now?

When I had lit my cigarette, that was when I had begun to hear voices. The first time I thought it was the porter, but had it been? And now it was this woman. Could a man listen to the thoughts of others? Did these cigarettes allow that to happen?

I looked back at the woman. I put the roll of paper to my lips. When the smoke was pulled into my lungs, I felt a rush of something. It was cold, a tingle like ants' feet scattering over my tongue.

"No, no," I repeated. "This isn't my home. My home's west of here. I live on the coast actually. Is this your home?"

"Don't tell him yet."

"No."

"Where then?"

"He lives out west. Tell him that you live east—somewhere where he's never been before."

"I live in Königsberg," she said.

"Beautiful city," I replied and leaned my back against the railing. This was amazing. Time to probe a little deeper. A little lie wouldn't go amiss.

"I have a cousin that lives there. A representative in the local assembly. Unhinged. He's a socialist after all, trying to cram reforms through the legislature. I think he writes a new proposal every weekend, but a good man nonetheless."

"This man here is a conservative, too. He could be a good match. Say that you don't understand why the socialists are so obsessed with the social order. See what he says."

"I just don't understand why the socialists want to change everything. I mean, what is wrong with the way things are?"

My thoughts were bustling. "All things are established for a reason," I said flatly.

"He's a good match. Invite him to sit with you. He doesn't seem that bad a character. Maybe your brother will like him."

"I think the train's speeding up," she said, glancing back over the railing. We were crossing a bridge and moving on into the countryside. "Where are you going?"

"Istanbul." I smiled. "I'm going all the way."

"Would you like to sit with me and my brother? Or do you have your seat already?"

I could not let this go, not yet. "Oh, that doesn't matter. I'll be happy to join you if your brother allows me."

"*Good. Now reel him in.*" She went to the door of the car and opened it.

"Compartment number four. My name is Anya." She smiled shyly. "What's yours?"

"Mark."

"It's good to meet you, Mark. I'll see you soon." She ducked inside and slid the door closed.

She was gone. The ash was flying every which way.

"By God," I said out loud, amazed. "It works! I'm really hearing her thoughts. I really think these work…" I checked the pack. There were nine sticks left. I took another puff and laughed to myself. Clairvoyant. I could barely believe it. It *had to be* the cigarettes!

Returning to my compartment, I felt like a nabob, a pasha of the world. If what I expected was true, I had everything and everyone in the palm of my hand, and I owed it to myself to use them. I had it all in my head, you see. I could go, undermine my competitor as easy as the devil, and, all the while, I would look as if I were only smoking my morning cigarette. If I could read their minds, it would be all be so easy. I could do anything I pleased... anything.

I took my suitcase from the luggage rack and picked up my briefcase before I noticed the other suitcase that sat at the foot of the opposite seat. My neighbor had forgotten it in his rush. Considering it for a moment, I took one last puff before I crushed the butt of the cigarette in the little ceramic ashtray below the window.

"Come on now. You know you want to look inside it."

I stopped. The voice was different than before, deeper than that girl's. I looked around and even out into the corridor to see if anyone was passing by, but I was alone. I looked back at the suitcase. Could I be reading my own mind? No, I hadn't had the thought to look in the suitcase. I shook my head. Maybe it was my subconscious.

"*Don't lie to yourself. Come on... Maybe there are some more of those cigarettes in it?*"

The hair on the back of my neck raised.

"Who's there?"

"*Oh... now you recognize me,*" came the reply. The words were like ice. "*Didn't hear me before? Don't be afraid. I won't lead you wrong. I'm your...* conscience. *Your inner light.*" The voice was getting harder to hear over the sound of the train, the hissing syllables sliding over one another and mingling with the mechanical noise of the locomotive.

"Where are you?" I asked, my mouth suddenly dry. I thought I was going insane. That voice... It grated, it scraped, and it scrabbled over my brain. Shivers trickled down my spine. At first, it sounded as if whatever it was had been right up against my ear, but now it had faded completely away. I stood there, straining to hear, every inch of myself stretching taught, ready to snap in a moment.

Nothing. There was nothing but the sound of the locomotive.

What now? I was left there, in that room that felt so intolerably small and cramped with a voice that was not my own parading in my head.

I rummaged for another cigarette, counting carefully: Eight, plus the one I now rolled between my fingers, made nine. Good. I snatched the matchbook, then swore. My hands were trembling so bad that twice I dropped the damn match when it flared up. I had to stomp each one out, which made tiny scorch marks in the carpet. Finally, the little lucifer caught the cigarette, and I took a deep drag. I waited for the drug, or whatever it was, to take hold and hopefully hear those voices again.

Then, imperceptibly at first, the tingle crept across my tongue, and again, that almost cool sensation oozed over me. This time it did nothing to steady my hands, so I waited in a plume of my own smoke.

I checked my watch. I took another puff.

"Alright," I said. "I don't know who you are, but this isn't funny, understand? Whatever game you're playing, it isn't funny. I won't have it, I tell you." Again, nothing. I pointed at the window with the cigarette, shaking my head at my own distorted reflection. The glass, strangely flawed, made my head look warped like someone had put a dent in my brow with a hammer. Another moment, and then another, before I breathed a heavy sigh. I didn't hear anything. I suppose it was just someone in the adjoining compartment. That was all... Or someone passing by, even though I had seen nobody. Still, it had to be someone talking, someone passing by. It *had* to be.

Well, no matter, I thought, clinching the cigarette between my teeth while I took up my bags. I lifted my hat from the hook by the door and headed toward Anya's suite.

"There you are!" she said and stood up. She was opposite from a man in whiskers, who must have been her brother. "Georg, this is the man I told you about. He's on his way to Istanbul like us, and I thought he wouldn't mind some company along the way."

"Very well," said the brother. He folded his newspaper across his knee but refused to stand.

"Beel. Mark Beel," I said by way of introduction. I shook his hand after I had set down my briefcase.

"Georg Harsch," said the brother. He leaned back to observe, adjusting his tight collar. "And I see you have already met Anya." I smiled, nodded, and sat down next to the woman.

"Yes, yes," I said and took the little ashtray from the window. I knocked off the ash from the cigarette. "She was kind enough to talk to me while I was having a smoke break on the observation platform."

"Quite."

"Mark actually knows something about psychology," she said. She used my name as if she were already intimately acquainted with it.

"Do you?" asked the brother, eyeing me. His brow was furrowed, dark hair combed back severely from his forehead. It looked as if he had combed it with a ten-penny-nail instead of the fine tooth, ivory handled comb I saw protruding from his breast pocket.

"Damn sister. She's such a flirt, and no mistake. Always has been." This voice was distinctly higher pitched, whiny, more like the buzz of a gnat than an actual voice. It was not like the girl's, which had been silent on the matter.

"Are you a psychologist, sir?" asked Georg.

"No, no," I said. "I'm a salesman of a kind."

"A salesman? What kind of man is that? You knew a salesman not too long ago, and he cheated you out of a good chunk of money."

"What kind of salesman exactly, sir?"

"I am an insurance broker for my firm, sir," I said, reaching into my pocket for my card case.

"I swear, if he reaches for his card, you would be well within your rights to strangle him!" I paused, fumbled, and took out my ticket which the conductor had punched. The now hazy air curled lazily around me while I pretended to fan myself with the paper.

"You, uh, don't mind if I smoke, do you?" I asked.

"No," came Anya's immediate response.

"Not at all," said Georg.

"Damn libertines. Why do they always have to smoke in your face like that? Always so full of themselves, as if they're the only ones that matter. You should throw him off the train or bash his head out with your cane." I looked to see a slim cane with a golden head cast in the shape of a dog's. I didn't say a word and let the noise of the train fill the gaps of the conversation.

"You said you were an insurance broker," Georg said. He fingered the head of the cane before he set it down across his lap. I gave a sigh of relief. For a moment, he looked like he was actually going to lift up that cane and brain me with it.

"To hell with you, Georg. Coward! I knew you didn't have the guts to act, much less be a broker. You have the opportunity to

make the world a better place, one without bastards like this crowding in. The world's getting too full nowadays anyway, so what are you doing? Nothing! You're weak, a two-timing, penny-licking bastard. Skipping out on the court fees, is that it? Don't want to pay daddy's lawyer? Shows what kind of man you are. A brat. A prig. A two-faced son-of-a-bitch."

"Yes," I said, hesitantly. Perhaps, just maybe, what I was hearing was his subconscious. Although, if I was honest with myself, I didn't know what to think exactly.

Then I heard the woman's inner voice.

"He's nervous. Why is he so nervous? Is that a new cigarette? You knew men smoked, but do they really indulge that much? It would be ridiculous if he smoked that much. You will have to fix that in the courtship. You do not want someone that can't control their appetites. Otherwise, you'll be unable to keep him reigned in."

"What?" I asked, startled, looking over to Anya, who was picking at the fingers of her gloves.

"I didn't say anything," she started. "Why? What is it?"

"He's jumpy," said the brother's inner voice. *"Why? Ask him why."* I looked to the brother, who had reopened his newspaper. There was a headline about a murder that had taken place half a

world away, and right next to that, an advertisement for the finest goats-hair wigs.

"It's nothing," I said. "I just thought I heard something, is all." I tried my best to smile.

"They can tell you're lying," came a sing-song voice, the same that he had heard in his old compartment. The train rattled.

"I'm sorry," I said, barking the phoniest laugh I had ever given. "I think I forgot something in my seat."

"Good, he's gone," came Georg's inner voice. He turned a page in his paper, not saying a word.

"Don't let him go. He may be your last chance at a good match, you know, and if you let him go, you'll be an old maid like Aunt Alice."

"Don't be long!" said Anya as the door closed.

I left my bags. I had to get out of there. Those voices were crowding in on me. I unbuttoned my coat and worked at my tie to get it loose. No one was walking through the corridor then, no conductor, no porters, no other passengers, just me. I put my hand under my hat and ran fingers through my hair. I could not understand it. The voices I was hearing, or *thought* I was hearing, could only be delusions, but they were so... *real*. I could not explain it away. I took the cigarette out of my mouth and held it up and really examined it for the first time. White paper curled and blackened with the little fire, turning to stinking ash. It was a smell I thought I had grown used to.

"Have you ever considered that this is something new?"

"Dammit, who's there?" I blurted, glancing around.

"Have you ever once considered that this is, perhaps, something you've never experienced before? Ever consider that this is something that can look like an ordinary thing, but is, in reality, something that you never thought was possible? Something very real?"

"What are you talking about?" I asked, and then I laughed. I was talking with myself! What kind of insanity was that? If anyone had seen me at that moment, they'd want to put me in an asylum.

"You're not insane, Mark. Believe me, I would know. You are quite sane."

"And how would you know that?" I walked down the corridor. While I paced, I felt the speed of the train through the rattle of the tracks beneath my shoes.

"You forget your lessons really easily, don't you?" laughed the voice. It was something like a knife keening over a whetstone, harsh and cold. *"I'm your inner light. I tell you when other people*

are lying, when you're lying to yourself—You're welcome by the way. It's a rather simple concept to get through your brain, but I suppose you need to have someone walk you through it, don't you?"

"That doesn't help me, whatever you are."

"Sure it does."

I balled up my fists. "Then what the hell are you?"

"Oh! He's a clever boy, isn't he?"

"What do you mean?"

"Next stop! Next stop!" The conductor called, having just entered the car. As he worked his way down the corridor, he was trumpeting in a way that only auction callers, preachers, and railway conductors could.

The pace of the train slowed. I ducked into my old compartment and sat down next to that abandoned suitcase, all that was left of my old traveling companion.

"Do you know how much fun this is for me?" came the voice conspiratorially, as if it were confiding in me.

"What in the hell do you mean?"

"There! He said it again!" the voice squealed. *"I tell you I have not had this much fun in a long time, Mark. Oh, I'll have fun with you, make no mistake about that. Just you wait. I have some surprises in store for you."*

"I *can't* be talking to myself," I said, rubbing my temples.

"*What gave you that idea? I certainly didn't give it to you. You came up with that yourself. You and your psychology.*" The brakes squealed as the train came to a complete stop. "*Here,*" said the voice, "*since you're going to throw away these cigarettes after you finish this last one, I'm going to give you a little hint as to what I am. Hm? Will that help you, Mark? Will that put your little scientific mind at ease?*"

I looked at the last little bit of the cigarette. "I'm talking with a voice in my head," I said to myself.

"*Yes, you are. So?*" The train was sliding into the station. "*Come on... You know you want to do it. To know for certain exactly what I am. Ask me a question, any question.*"

"Can I ever get rid of you? Are you always going to be there?"

"*Oh, Mark, you are simple, aren't you? I said, one question, but you asked two. I know you had a hard time in arithmetic when you were younger, but honestly, this is just pathetic. But, since you are being such a meek little boy, I'll answer both. I'll be with you wherever you go. Just know that I am never totally gone, even when you can't hear me. Fortunately for us, you're never quite free.*"

"Us?"

"Oh yes. Us. As in a multitude. Masses."

"So, you are not part of the brain? A part of my mind?"

"*No, thank you,*" said the voice, sounding exasperated. "*I'm very thankful that I am not a part of that rat's nest. It's a rather disgusting proposition if you ask me, almost obscene. I am my own creature, thank you very much.*"

I took one last drag, all the way down to the last scrap of tobacco.

"Are you some kind of magician? Is this something like telepathy? I've seen some street magicians use it on people—"

"*No. I'm not. What magician uses telepathy? Really, Mark, you're better than this. You remind me of that exorcist.*"

"Are you a hallucination then?"

"*Asking a hallucination for information? I had you pegged for at least a marginally intelligent man, Mark. Shame on you for letting me down. Just think about it. Mark Beel having a conversation with a chair or an icebox. Now that's an amusing picture, I can tell you.*"

"What—" I choked, trying not to scream. "What—are—you?" I stood bolt upright, fists shaking.

I threw the butt of the cigarette to the floor. Above the seat opposite me, there was a mirror that stretched along the back of the cabin from the wall with the door, over to the window. I saw myself in that mirror and the beads of sweat running off the end of my nose. My eyes bulged. Every hair stood on end while I stared at myself, eyes wider than they had ever gone, drinking the light that came from the outside. I tasted iron in my mouth.

Since the train had finally come to a stop, I saw people walk along the station platform. There was a general shuffling of humanity as passengers filed down the center passageway.

"Mark," came the voice, gravelly. It pronounced every word with precision, as if they were measured and cut from a bolt of cloth: "*I am not an illusion or some conjurer's trick. I am not an imbalance of your brain chemistry, though, after this, you will try to tell yourself that. I am not some part of your runaway imagination or a simple ringing in your ear. There is nothing simple about me. To call myself simple is to do a disservice to myself and my purpose. My purpose, Mark Beel, is to know you better than you know yourself. My purpose is to give you purpose, to guide you along whatever path is set in front of you.*" The voice was fainter now, growing muddled by the noise of people calling to one another.

"*Those sudden thoughts that you have, those tricky little ideas that always seem to sneak up on you out of the blue? Those are because of me, Mark. I am the voice in the dark. I am the one that lets you see the truth behind things, pushes you toward the end that lights your way. That's what I am, Mark. And you and I, oh the things we will do together... the works... oh... We will have a devil of a time!*"

Like that, the voice was gone, leaving me alone in the train car. I stared at my reflection. I stepped back and nearly tripped over the suitcase. I sat down, hands by my side, the old leather-bound case between my knees. I looked up at the ceiling of the suite, at the designs that writhed themselves into snakes, some devouring others whole. My hand flew to the pack that was still in my pocket, next to my train ticket. I pulled out the bright red box and looked at it, read the bold, white lettering beneath the eyes that stared out from golden circles when, suddenly, a feeling crept up on me that the eyes would move if I stared at them long enough. I dropped the pack and let it fall on the top of the suitcase.

I put my head in my hands.

I didn't want to think. I didn't want to feel anything else at that moment. An empty mind was all I wanted. Not this confused jumble that I was left with, not with this panic, this anxiety that cloyed. Those ideas and what I had thought of myself were shrinking and felt as if they were being pressed down between two glass panes, drained of their color. Now they seemed as flat to me as any worn-out picture, as lifeless as any dead man.

"Good afternoon," came a voice cheerfully. "Do you mind if I sit with you?"

I looked up, saw a man, with a small suitcase in one hand and an umbrella in the other. He had a smile on his face and a scarf wound tight around his neck. I looked away and out the window. There wasn't a cloud in the sky.

"Say," he said, tilting his head. "I can leave if you don't want any company. I just figured since you were sitting by yourself..."

"Not at all. Please," I said and indicated the opposite seat.

"Thank you, thank you," said the young man and put up his luggage. When he sat down, he patted his coat and then his pants. "Well damn," he said, with a smile. "It seems as if I smoked my last. Got a smoke?"

I looked at that young man dead in the eyes. I did not blink. I did not think.

I only spoke.

Noah W. Newmann

At the Crossroads of Oldforge Gibbet

ONCE THERE WAS A PILGRIM who stopped at a crossroads in the middle of a great wood at dusk. This man, who was at the end of his days, stood stock still and listened to the creaking of a rope. His liver-spotted hand clutched a walking staff that was almost as gnarled and knobby as he. He was far from any town, alone, and very weary. The forest grew around the road, and the gloam of twilight caught the sky above. Fireflies spun lazily, looping on themselves in flight between the tangled branches of the wood. To his left, at the edge of the curtain of trees, from the end of a gibbet that was overgrown with a tangle of thorns, another man dangled. He was long dead, and the stir of the wind clattered his bones. On the shoulder of the dead man, there perched a jackdaw. Its head tilted to one side to show its big, shining eye.

Seclusion, the feeling of secrecy, deadened the air. Creeping roots crowded the cobbled path, and ancient trunks in their jackets of peeling, curling bark, walled in the Pilgrim. Branches, draped with long moss, locked together overhead, nearly blocking out the sky. Men rarely, if ever, witnessed such an intimacy of time and place. Here the Pilgrim stood, smelling of the outer world with dust on his feet and clothes he had worn to the barest of threads. He looked up.

Eyes peered back at him from the tree that stretched high into the sky, up out of the ground, a living pillar. In the gloom, the light of the fireflies outlined a face, a figure, wrought massive, nearly giant. It was fixed in its seat, as if the roots of the great tree were its throne and the mossy boulders its footstool. Like a prince, it sat. A voice, profound and deep rumbled from the figure.

"And what, good traveler, will be your final wish?"

The Pilgrim blinked when he met the eyes of the figure. He looked about him, at the trees, the two paths diverging, the jackdaw that spied on him from the shoulder of the dead man, and at Venus shining in her heaven.

"Where am I?" asked the Pilgrim in a trembling voice. His eyes darted back and forth, and the grip on his staff grew lax. The scent of moss and mold drifted down from the trees and soured the roof of his mouth. "I have no memory of this place. I don't know why I'm here. I don't know who I am. Who are you, stranger? What has happened to me?"

The figure at the base of the tree tilted its head.

"You, good traveler, are at the crossroads. You have journeyed here from a far land, across the ocean where men, in their wisdom, have thought of better things to do than to search out places like this—or things like me. But you came in search of a legend, good traveler. You came in search of me, he whom people call the 'Djinn of the Crossroads.'"

The figure bore up in his seat, great hands, vices, gripping the roots until he stood. His head bent beneath the dark canopy of the tree. Behind him, pearlescent feathers caught the last of evening's gloom, wings stretched out to either side.

"You have passed every trial in your search of me," continued the Djinn. "With every ounce of your energy, you sought me. As your reward, you have found me. Wishes three do I give to the one who seeks and finds—myself made a slave to the finder's own will, until my obligation is fulfilled. Here are the laws of the seeker's wish: I cannot make anyone fall in love, nor can the finder wish for more wishes. Those are the stipulations.

These are the laws of my enslavement. I have accomplished both the first and second of your three wishes. Now I wait for you to speak your last and thus free me from my bondage. That is what has happened to you. That is who people say I am. That is the moment." The figure was monumental. Eyes stared at the Pilgrim, shining like coins.

"What, then, was my second wish?" asked the Pilgrim, shifting his staff from one hand to the other. His fingers worried the knots in the wood.

"To forget yourself," said the Djinn. "'Let every memory be washed from my mind,' you said. 'Let my very self dissolve. Who I am and who I was and my purpose.' So you wished, and so I granted."

The Pilgrim searched his mind, testing to see if what the Djinn said was true. He looked behind himself to see footprints—his own—fade into the dust of the path and the dark of the forest. Above him, the moon, slender and sharp, slid over the velvet sky. He felt suddenly older than the oldest city. His bones were made of something like the columns of a Pompeiian temple, wrapped in ash. He felt the ghosts of all his forgotten yesterdays gather together in his joints, crying out against the possibility of him facing so many tomorrows without their doleful company.

He gripped his staff and straightened his back. His bald pate glistened with a sheen of sweat, and his breath came fast. He was a human being, a man that had not traveled to this place to be robbed of his own self by his own hand. What memories had been lost with that most recent wish? What moments of childhood destroyed? For all he knew, he had family, children, friends. He had a life, but how could he call his life his own if he did not even know it? Who would welcome home? To what government would he give his allegiance? What god? He felt at the ragged edges of his soul, the patches torn from his mind, and resolved himself, gathered up his will.

"Then I have a new wish for you, Djinn," said the Pilgrim. He planted his staff in the dirt. His former wish was foolish. He would make it right. "I wish to know myself. I wish to know who I truly am!"

When the Djinn seated himself back on the roots of the great tree, the Pilgrim saw the Djinn's face clearly for the first time. It was cut from ancient marble. His eyes were a maelstrom of variegated color, and his lips had the curve of temptation. He waved a hand as if he were swatting away a fly.

"Good traveler, your wish is granted! And by my doing so, I am freed. Thank you."

As he spoke, the Djinn melted into the twilight like a mirage. A wind then arose from the belly of the forest and pulled at the Pilgrim's cloak. The Djinn's voice raised over the sudden noise.

"But I find it funny, good traveler. *That* was your first wish."

In a moment, the Djinn was gone. At the edge of hearing, there was the cawing of the jackdaw and the clack of bones. All about the Pilgrim, the light had gone, leaving him alone in a night without borders—an endless dark.

An Interesting Hypothesis

"Precinct 31 receiving. Over."

The detective could hear that the dispatcher was tired through the static of the car radio. The detective's partner, sent out that morning from the station, stood nearby the patrol car and tucked his hands into jacket pockets. All around them, snow sugared the city, and there was no traffic. The detective adjusted the radio to clear the interference.

"Yes. This is Detective Surroe. I would like to report a missing vehicle. Over."

"Go ahead, Detective. Over."

"Vehicle was last seen parked outside of the West Corner Inn and Bar on the Reau de St. Merced at approximately twenty-one hundred hours. Description is a maroon public service vehicle. License plate is 6M-04."

The detective heard a tearing sound from the radio receiver, like ripping paper. After a second, the dispatcher cleared the static from his throat.

"Who is reporting the missing vehicle? Over."

"I am. Over."

"We will start our inquiry straight away, Detective. Thank you for informing us." A chair's clatter and an office door's slam delivered feedback through the receiver. The detective winced and drew back. His headache was painful enough.

A new voice demanded, "Who's on the line?"

It was growling, muffled. Surroe recognized the voice and closed his eyes to toss a prayer to whomever might be listening. He could already see the man's patchy beard and heavy eyebrows scowling across the dispatcher's desk. It was not pleasant.

"Detective Surroe, sir," the dispatcher intoned flatly.

"What has he gone and done now?"

"He is reporting a missing vehicle, sir."

"Oh, is he?"

The mic squealed when the new man snatched it up from its stand. The pain in Surroe's head flared, making him feel as if an interrogation lamp were blinding him. The voice snarled through the radio.

"What's the description of the vehicle, Detective?"

Surroe opened his eyes. No one was taking prayers, apparently.

"Good morning, Sergeant Mac. Over."

"Yeah yeah, lovely weather. What's the description of that missing vehicle?"

"Sergeant," said the dispatcher, a little muffled now, "the description he gave is here."

"Let me see that." Static played. Surroe's partner, several feet away, kicked at a snow drift, spilling the grayish slush from the curb into the street. The voice of the sergeant crackled over the speakers again. "Is the license plate number I'm reading correct, Detective?"

"If it's the one I gave the dispatcher, yes, sir. It is. Over."

"Isn't that *your* plate number, Detective?"

"Yes, sir. It is. Over."

"You mean to tell me that you lost your department vehicle."

"I did not lose it, sir. It got stolen. Over."

"And what? You weren't going to tell us?"

"I just did, sir. Over."

A muffled and rattle passed through the radio as if someone on the other end suddenly stood up.

"I'll go and put this in the grand theft auto list, then," said the dispatcher, voice growing more faint as he leaves the range of the mic.

Surroe's superior roared. "Unbelievable! How did it get stolen, Detective? Did you leave it unlocked? Where are your car keys? What the hell were you thinking?"

"Sir, I'll tell you what happened—"

"Please do, Detective. I would really love to know what to put in the report so that everyone knows exactly how Michael Surroe botched the whole goddamn investigation because I bet he spent too much money on booze. *Again*."

The detective lifted a shaking hand to his head, pain sizzling behind his eyes.

"It's not quite like that, sir. I conducted the initial rounds of the investigation, staked out the premises, and all seemed fairly normal. Nothing suspicious, and, well, damn me if someone picked my pocket while I was asking questions around the bar. I woke up in the morning in the hotel to find that my keys were missing and my car was gone. That's my story. Over."

"That's your story? Then how in blazes are you calling in?"

"I'm calling from my partner's car radio, sir. He just came over this morning, about fifteen minutes ago. Over." Surroe's partner looked up from the frozen curb toward his open car door.

"Unbelievable. Simply…" Interference overwhelmed the Sergeant's rant. "…I'll have patrol alerted to look for your *missing* vehicle. Is there anything else you need to report, Detective?"

"No, sir. Over."

"I want to see you when you get back to the station, Surroe. I'll be staying late, *just for you*."

"I'm looking forward to it, sir. Over."

"Over and out. *Piece of—*" The line chirped, then died, and Surroe hung the mic on the dashboard. He nudged the door shut with his hip as his partner made his way over to him. The detective buttoned his policeman's coat.

"So they're going to alert patrol to look for the car?" asked his partner. "I don't think that's going to help all that much, especially in this neighborhood." He looked up at the surrounding tenements, their crumbling façades and the mounds of dirty snow that almost obscured the gang tags.

"It won't," said Surroe. "It's not because of the neighborhood, though."

"Then why won't they find your car then?"

Surroe shivered. "Damn, it's cold. Got a nip?"

"Sure. Here."

Surroe took the flask from his partner, then a swallow from the flask. He did not give it back.

"Thank you. *God,* this hangover... And that call didn't help in the slightest."

"How much did you drink, Mike?"

"I had to go undercover for the case, have a few drinks, play a game of cards—the whole schtick. Had a few bad hands, too. Good chunk of money and... well." The two followed the sidewalk, the crackling ice spider-webbing out from their winter boots.

Surroe's partner stopped. The detective continued on for a few paces before turning back on his heel.

"No..." said his partner. "You didn't. You didn't! I know you... You wouldn't go that far."

Surroe crossed his arms.

"You got in too deep, didn't you, Mike? You put the keys of your car in the pot. *That's* what you did, isn't it?"

Surroe took another swallow from the flask and tucked it into his jacket philosophically. He considered the sky and the snow that was just then beginning to fall from the January gray.

"That's... an interesting hypothesis."

Noah W. Newmann

Le Révolutionnaire

It was June the seventh, 1832, and, once again, the revolution in Paris had failed. Renee sat in the aftermath of this failure on a cane-back chair, looking worn, his military coat draped loosely about his shoulders, an officer's sword resting at his hip. His shako hat stood tall beside the chair as if to keep watch while Renee held a small leather book open in his hands. Careless for all except his reading, he licked his thumb and turned a page.

Outside, on the avenue, soldiers moved back and forth from the barricade that squatted in the middle of the street. They carried bits of it with them: chairs, tables, even carriage wheels. Like blue and white coated ants, they went, either to the waggoneers that would carry the rubbish somewhere outside the city, or to one of the many fires that surrounded the barricade.

Wind pulled the smoke, which was oily and dark, across the fronts of the dwellings, blacking white plaster fronts freckled with bullet holes.

Renee's chair was set in the deserted parlor on the first floor of one such tenement since there was nothing left in the whole house. The young and reckless, who had taken this particular boulevard, had snatched up everything. They had shattered the front window and long since gathered the entry door to the barricade. Now, another man leaned against the doorframe, his figure haloed in the morning light, even as his chin rested against his lieutenant's uniform.

"*This is our Calvary,*" said Renee dramatically, almost to himself.

"Pardon?" said the lieutenant, instantly snapping awake. Renee held up the book and tapped a line on a page.

"It is something that our friend wrote in his diary."

"About what, exactly?"

"Oh, about this whole affair." Renee sighed, flipping back in the little book while his eyes scanned the lines of a young man's hurried hand. "Ah yes!" he said and set his finger under the first lines of an entry dated May. "*'The day is coming soon when we will call each man brother and citizen, without fear of sup-*

pression or violence, when all of France will unite under the old banners of Liberty, Egality, and Fraternity. This is our Calvary.' You know, he's quite poignant at times."

"Mm," grunted the lieutenant. Once again, he rested his chin on his chest and propped a boot on the doorframe. "He would have done better to stay locked up in his rooms."

"Maybe," said Renee, somewhat distracted. "That does not take away his point, does it? His ideals, I mean. True, he was a student, but..."

"I do not know what you mean," the lieutenant barked, exasperated. "He should have continued to study law or whatever it was that he did."

"He studied medicine at the Hôtel Dieu, I think."

"Medicine then! He should have become a doctor and not a revolutionary. But no! He decides to become an idealogue and die with a bullet through the eye. These idiots are always reading their books, extolling the heroism of the revolution, and they say 'Liberty! Give us liberty!' without any notion of what they are actually saying."

"And what is it that they are saying, Lieutenant?"

"They are saying that everything that was done in the past means nothing!" exclaimed the lieutenant, straightening his uniform. "They say that the king is nothing but a tyrant when all he has done for the country is pour out his soul for his people. Under the rule of kings, our nation conquered the world, but they shrug it off as merely an accident of history. *The Revolution,* they declare, *made us great* when it was only senseless murder of the royalty.

"They are hoping for a day when men and women will turn on one another again! Butcher each other and crucify their neighbors, send them to Madame Guillotine for treason against another 'republic.' They forget their station. That is all the revolutionary hopes for, my captain. Liberty is cruel and only gives what she can take. They had three days of *glory* behind their barricade. And now," the lieutenant spat, "for me, I am glad that he is dead."

Renee continued to study the diary and turned another page. Somewhere outside the townhouse, on the boulevard, a soldier called out to one of his comrades and laughed. There was a sound of splintering wood and the whoosh of sparks when another bulwark of the revolution went up in flames.

"Were you alive during 'the Terror,' Lieutenant?" asked Renee.

"No, sir."

"Well, I was. A little boy maybe but still alive." Renee looked up from the pages of the diary, out the broken window through which he saw a scavenger pick up a stove and heave it onto his cart. "It was as you say," observed Renee. "Bloody and chaotic. But it was life back then. The world seemed mad, turned upside down and shaken about without any sense to it." He paused, reached up, and scratched the bridge of his nose. He let his hand fall but kept peering into the rafters.

"Do you go to church, Lieutenant?"

"Eh?"

"Do you go to church?"

"No, sir."

"Well... I used to go with the parish priest, Père Innocence, with all of my family, my sisters, brothers, their children, even my grandparents before they passed. Why don't you go?"

The lieutenant shrugged. "It never occurred to me to go. It seemed rather pointless. I was christened like everyone else, which was good enough for me."

"You would say that," said Renee after a chuckle. He looked back at the diary. "Well, it seems that our little revolutionary here was a true believer."

"Was he now?" The lieutenant rolled his eyes. "And what visions did our 'friend' have since he was so pious?"

"No, no visions per sé, only prayers. You see, he wrote the initials at the top of many of the pages: A.M.D.G. They're Latin, you know. 'For the greater glory of God.' Though he did write under that the initials, 'S.D.G.' Perhaps he was confused..."

"Why is that?"

"Nothing, Lieutenant. You would not understand, still... Here, let me read to you what he wrote. This is an entry from March of this year: *'I went into prayer today. Always when I prayed, I felt like I was doing something wrong. Likewise, I came to the confessional, and I was weary with myself, and, in my heart, I felt a sickness, a weight that was very much real. Like lead, it pressed me down. The priest at the university used to give me prayers to say. For each sin, five Hail Mary's and five Our Father's. I would pray them gladly, in cycle, for it was a good exercise, I think. Still, that weight would never quite leave me.*

'I am indebted, however, to the priest in my home village for his attention to me. A gentle and kind man, he would pray with me. A very holy man who, in fact, baptized me. I went into prayer with him today in the garden of the old abbey of his order, and he laid his hand on my shoulder afterward and spoke to me. Then, I

wept, and, for the first time in my life, I felt as if I could indeed call a man my father. The weight is gone from me. I have entered through the gates of Heaven. Glory be to God.'" Renee paused in his reading and looked up at the lieutenant, smiling curiously. "Interesting, isn't it?"

The lieutenant crossed his arms. "He had a guilty conscience. All the religious do. Self-flagellation to a God they cannot see—stupid. I would wager that he was deluded in his own ideals, would critique himself to death if you would let him, and that he exploited his frustration with this stupid little *riot*. He was nothing but a sycophant, a want-to-be doctor that holidayed as a theologian. No wonder he got shot through the brain. It was a mercy."

"What I mean," Renee cut in, leafing again through the diary, "is that he was something of an idiot with how he thought religion works. I won't deny it. *But,* that does not rid him of his morals. From what I see, aside from a night of drinking with university friends and the whole revolution affair, he seemed to be a good lad. Full of promise, I would say. Reminds me of my nephew..." Renee trailed off.

"Your nephew?"

"What? Uh, yes. He would be twenty now, in school, studying hard. He wants to become a soldier like his father, but we all say no. No, you will become a doctor. The world needs good doctors, no matter what other people say about them. I don't think he believes me, but what else is an uncle there for, other than to put his nephew on the right path, eh?" He shrugged, his massive coat nearly falling from his shoulders.

"I suppose," said the lieutenant, looking out at the boulevard and the soldiers moving back and forth. "Captain, don't you think we've kept the colonel waiting long enough?"

"Let us read the last entry, alright? It's the least we can do. We will consider it as his last testament, Lieutenant. We can give the boy that much respect, can't we?"

The lieutenant let his head fall back so that his shako bumped up against the frame of the door, pushing the visor down over his eyes. Renee barked a laugh and flipped to the last few pages of the diary.

In the first half of the little book, the letters had been watery, poorly formed. Entries sometimes came months apart. Then the entries became more uniform, the style more genuine. Now the penmanship was mature, no longer a boy's but a man's. Renee traced the date of the last entry, the sixth of June, '32, and began to read aloud.

"*'I am at my post, two pistols in my belt, a dagger in my boot, and a musket on my shoulder. I see the soldiers gather on the other side of the barricade. No cavalry this time.*

"*'There will be a night attack, but there is a fear that rises in my belly. It comes from the knowledge that we will not be able to hold, that this will be our last stand. The more I contemplate this fear, the more I find that I cannot say that what we have done here is completely right, though it is certainly not wrong. But what have we done it for? Freedom from a tyranny only we can see? The people of Paris do not unite under our banner as we thought they would. Instead, they leave the fight for the cause to us... while they wait to see which way the cat jumps. I cannot help but see our gesture as futile.'*"

"Sounds to me like he was beginning to come to his senses."

"That is enough, Lieutenant," said Renee, turning the page. He continued: "*'No. I am not happy. But this is my place, and this is my charge. We are committed, and I am resigned to my duty with every ounce of my strength. I must keep in mind that I do not fight for myself. I, along with my comrades, fight for all the people of France. But also, I fight for another, for her. Perhaps I will see her again, after all this is done.*

'The evening draws to a close. I hear church bells toll from every quarter of the city. They are ringing Vespers.'"

Renee closed the diary.

"So..." said the lieutenant. "He was an idiot after all. And just when I was beginning to take a liking to him."

"I do not deny it," sighed Renee, shouldering into his uniform coat. "And I agree with you. We've kept the colonel waiting long enough. Besides, there is seldom any profit in dwelling on the past."

"Yes, sir," grunted the lieutenant. His buckle and buttons clacked against the bayonet dangling at his hip as the lieutenant patted the doorframe goodbye.

The two made their way out of the building's shade and into the sun. The lieutenant fell in line behind his superior, passing through the lines of scavengers and the occasional soldier. They detoured around one of the many fires that continually burned with the refuse piled there. Shattered framework tangled across a mountain of white-gray ash, and yellow flames jumped up from their latest fuel. The sleeve of a dress coat hung out of a drawer, the gold brocade on the edge of the sleeve shriveling, twisting, dripping in a glitter on the ash.

Renee strode forward and shifted the diary from his left hand to his right, ready to toss it onto the blaze when his eye caught sight of something slipping from between the pages. It fluttered to the cobbles at his feet, catching his heel. Stopping, Renee reached down and took up a folded slip of paper from under his boot. He turned the paper over in his fingers and saw that it was tied with a thin, white ribbon.

"A letter?" grunted the lieutenant. "Probably from some strumpet he was seeing. Worthless, sir."

"Lieutenant?"

"Sir?"

"I left my shako beside the chair. Go fetch it for me."

The lieutenant hesitated, then saluted. "Yes, sir." Renee heard the lieutenant's boots scuff the cobbles, until they fade into the concert of street noise. Renee slid the ribbon off the square of paper gently, not wanting to damage it, and unfolded the letter. The handwriting was spidery and trembled across the page. The message read:

"*My Son,*

Your beloved is dying. There is no question. She is once again taken by the fever which grips over half our village, and her breath grows shallow. Come quickly, for her time is short. I will entrust this letter to the fastest messenger I can employ. If you can come, do so in all haste.

Finally, my son, I must share with you the words of your beloved, which she spoke to me after the anointing of oil. Here I record, faithfully, what Madeline insisted I write: 'My Jean. I know you are fighting for what you know to be right and good. So, you must stay there, and you must fight there. But when you do, do not forget my love.'

That was all that she said before she fell into a dream. Even now she sleeps. God keep you, my son. We all pray for your safe return.

—*Père Innocence.*"

Renee closed the letter and slipped the ribbon back over the square of paper. The old priest's letter had been dated the second of June, just a day before the uprising. Looking down, he flipped an ember back into the blaze with his boot. Gently, he tucked the letter back into the leaves of the diary and then the diary into the inside pocket of his jacket.

"Sir," said the lieutenant, who now stood beside Renee, his arm extended presenting the officer's shako. Renee buttoned the coat and accepted his hat. The lieutenant commented on something, but the captain did not hear him.

Renee stared at the wardrobe ablaze in the bonfire and saw the barricade loom behind like some evil mountain. The few revolutionaries that had been left after the siege had fought courageously against the royal soldier's final charge. Afterward, they were laid out like red jacketed fish, ready to be clapped into boxes and rolled away with the rest of the trash, but only after Renee's men had gutted them of anything valuable. Renee had been among his men, picking through the jackets of the young rebels for a ring or some spare change. While looting, he had taken the diary from the coat of a man he had shot.

At first, he had not recognized the finely featured young man with his bloody hair. Then his face had swum up to him out of the haze of smoke and memory, made suddenly and terribly real by the letter: a letter that bore the rickety writing of Renee's old parish priest. That young face now solidified itself in Renee's mind as the death mask of his nephew, Jean.

The lieutenant was still speaking, though Renee ignored him. Without a word, the captain took his shako, placed it upon his head, then buckled the strap under his chin and straightened his uniform. The lieutenant, sensing his captain's mood, stopped talking.

Before them, the bonfire, one of hundreds, burned on. They smelled the kindling of wood and cloth, the melting of lead, and the acrid scent of gunpowder. The wind shifted so that the columns of smoke, which rose languidly up into the sky, were pressed back between the high buildings, down into the boulevard. The two officers stood tall in their uniforms. Soldiers moved about them, most of them saluting when they passed, the habit of duty.

A horse drawing a cart clopped by, driven by a pale man with no chin. In the bed of the cart, three oblong boxes jostled, knocking against one another. The captain watched the cart turn down the road and trundle leisurely past another fire.

"Where is the colonel headquartered?" asked Renee in a low tone.

"Down the street there, some two hundred yards, sir." The lieutenant pointed down the street where the cart had gone.

"Then let us not waste any more time," said Renee, and he struck out across the boulevard, his hand on the pommel of his sword.

It Was Easier

IT WAS THE THIRTEENTH of September, and August J. Mallard was eighty-nine years old. He woke as he usually did, at four o'clock, before the stars had begun to blink out. No alarm or clock was needed to tell him the time because he knew it deep down in his bones. He had always said he could feel the time go by, like it was a thing out there in the world, speeding past him, a bus full of people.

"I have to get up," he would say, "and catch it before it goes off without me." Waking so early was a habit, and, like most habits, August did not want to break it.

He dressed in the glow of a coal-oil lamp. It was not that he did not like the convenience of electric light—he did have the entire house wired, after all—but he preferred this quiet, sputtering glow to the steady buzz of city-made bulbs. He only used the electric lights whenever the family came to visit. When they would pull up to the house, there the bulbs would be, humming away like stadium lamps. August would be standing there on the porch, waiting for the children, hands in his pockets, as if it were any other day of the week.

However, that day was not just any day. The children were staying at the house as part of a week-long trip, a rare and very special treat.

"Emma," he said. "I need you."

A voice would come floating up from the quilts in a whisper, still half-filled with sleep.

"What is it?"

"I need you to straighten my tie. I can't ever get it right." He would bring over the lamp which would cast his shadow over the ceiling. With a chink of brass, he would place it on the table, the better for her to see him.

"Get closer," she would chide, her voice having lost any trace of sleep. "And get down here so I can see you better."

"I'll have to bend over."

"If you have to, you have to. Do you want me to straighten your tie or not, old man?"

"But what if I can't straighten up?"

"Then I guess you'll just have to stay here, won't you?"

He would grumble a little more before he crouched over, joints popping like guitar strings. She would reach up, straighten the lopsided tie, and smooth his lapel. "You're wearing that jacket again?"

"What's wrong with it?"

"It has patches in the elbows."

"So? Gives the thing character, I think. Very professor-like."

"True, but ain't it kind of ratty?" she would ask.

"We have mice, Emma, not rats."

Laughter would come, a raspy, dry sound.

"Are you sure about the tie? It's straight and all, right? So I don't have to make a fool of myself in front of the children. Hat on straight, too?"

"Of course, it is. And the jacket looks very proper, very handsome." She would smile.

"Good morning, Emma."

"Good morning, dear. The dogs are barking outside. You want to take care of that 'fore they wake up the children or the grandbabies?"

"Of course, love."

This was how August J. Mallard would greet the day. Any other way was beyond him. There would be some variance in form, some change in order perhaps, like this day, when the dogs were making their racket out in the yard. It was a habit, and, like most habits, August did not want to break it.

August stood at the head of the stairs, one hand on the wall while the other held the lantern. He had forgotten his cane downstairs when he had gone to bed.

His son and his family were visiting, and the house, for once, was quiet. August's son, Ray, was sleeping in the in-law suite. He was with his bride and their two children, all nearly grown. They would always fret over August and fuss. They said stupid things, too. Useless things, like asking why he did not take the pills suggested by the specialist, or they would do things like leaving the latest health magazine for the elderly on the table. It was Ray's wife who was really worried.

Every time the family visited, August thanked God that he would wake up so early. At four o'clock, no one was stirring.

The dogs were barking.

His shadow from the lantern crept behind him down the stairwell, passing over the pictures that hung there. The first few steps were not so bad, and August began to think that the pain had gone away in the night. But on his third step, the bone began to bite. The pain flowed into a steady, crunching pressure. He put out his hand and traced the wall as a blind man would.

He remembered refusing to use the cane when Emma and the children had interrupted his breakfast by setting it by his chair. Its appearance had soured his glass of morning milk.

"I don't need that," he had harrumphed.

"Don't you harrumph at me, *old man*," Emma had said. "It's for your own good."

"It's doctor's orders, Pops," Ray had said, hands tucked into his pockets.

"It's to keep you safe, dear, so you don't hurt yourself. I want to keep you around as long as possible... Even if you are a crotchety old man."

"You're not much better yourself, *old woman*."

August had not been to a doctor's office since.

He stood on the landing in between the upstairs and the down. Outside, the dogs barked. August knew those barks, little puppy sounds almost. He smiled and made his way down the last few steps. The thoughts made it easier to ignore the hurt in his hip, which pulled the breath out of his chest with every second step.

Where was that cane again? Under the table or by one of the chairs? The dining room stretched ahead, long in the half-dark. Beyond the shadows, the windows looked onto the front porch, open. Cool air washed through the screens.

He knew that this was where he had left the thing, but where, exactly? Behind this chair? Over the back of another? Or maybe it was under the picture of him and Emma... no... not there either. Perhaps... August set the lamp on a corner of the table and went over to the bookshelf where, alongside the family bible, it lay where he had left it last night. He breathed a very deep, quiet sigh, feeling the pin-needle pain steadily recede when he set his weight over the thin shaft of oak.

Lantern in hand, August made his way across the dining room and opened the front door. His light streamed out onto the porch and beyond. At the far right, the glow of his lamp illuminated a ghostly fence, which separated his yard from the neighbor's cornfield. August whistled, and three pairs of eyes peeked from up behind the split rail fence.

"Go on!" August said in a harsh whisper. "Go on now! Git! We don't want to wake the children. Now git!" The dogs only stared at him, until one sneezed, and another hound yawned, his tongue a long, pink, wrinkled curl. "Oh, you boys," August muttered and closed the door behind him. He made his way over to his rocking chair and settled himself there.

He kept his eye on the dogs, lantern between his feet and cane hooked over the arm of his chair. They had quit their racket, which would usually disturb Emma most of all. He was sure they saw him as some strange, prehistoric creature emerging from a great, white-painted cave. He closed his eyes, laughing at the image. Emma would laugh at that, too, he was sure. He would have to remember to tell her.

The rocking chair creaked, and out there in the early morning, crickets chirped.

After living so long as an old man, August had acquired some skill at dozing, wrinkled hands laced over his belly.

On the porch, he dozed with his foot rocking him, light shining away. The lantern draped golden tendrils across the yard and against the fence. The dogs were spectators, wanting only to see what this pale creature, dressed in baggy clothes, would do. Maybe he was waiting for something. Sniffing each other, growling, nipping, yawning in one another's ears, the dogs counseled together on what they should do, and, in a vote that was decided two to one, settled down to wait on the old creature. They sat vigil for dawn, together with the chirruping of crickets.

It was a bit warmer than it normally was in September, but a cool breeze ruffled the tops of the stalks of corn, and, in the east, there was the faintest glimmer.

⚜   ⚜   ⚜

The dogs were barking.

August came to himself, suddenly awake. The dog that had nuzzled his palm jumped backward, barking, his claws scraping at the porch. The first thing that August saw was the sun blazing over the trees at the property line.

Dew sparkled blue on the grass, and the other two dogs barked as well. August's neck rolled, head spinning with the sudden noise. He heaved himself out of the rocking chair, took the weight on his hip, and reached out for one of the pillars of the porch. A dog slipped through his legs, panting.

"Get on! Get out!" he said and shooed them away. His vision spotted like a faulty film reel, each second like a frame so that his hand multiplied itself.

The house was awake. Voices chummed, younger and older together—Ray and the grandchildren. August knew that Ray would be at work in the kitchen with his wife, making their favorite meal. He smelled the sausage and the eggs and the coffee. He shook his head, dazed while dogs panted all around him. The lantern was dead and cold at the foot of the rocking chair.

"Hey there now. Hey there now," he said, looking to see one of the mutts slobbering over the cane he had hooked over the arm of the chair.

August moved to snatch the stick from the dog, but he was too slow. Before he could blink twice, the dog was off with his cane, wriggling under the fence and into the corn, the cane jutting ridiculously from both sides of his mouth. The other two mutts bounded after him with their own songs of jubilation.

"Hey there! Hey!" August called as he stepped out of the shade of the porch. His gate was uneven, stumbling, drifting. His ankle nearly twisted on the rutted turf of the yard, the grass and dandelions rising against him like a green and yellow army. They caught at the laces of his shoes and the cuffs of his pants, intent on not letting him go after the dog. To August's age-webbed eyes, the grass, indistinct and blurry as it was, could have been a scatter of barbed wire for all the trouble it gave him.

The dogs were *still* barking.

He looked at the fence, then over, out into the cornfield. He hated doing this. But it was what Emma wanted—him to be safe, and that cursed cane was one of those things that she believed kept him safe. His hip flared when he ducked under a rail and stepped into the cornfield.

The dogs were still barking but further away now.

Someone was calling from the house. August turned and saw Ray in that stupid canary-yellow shirt of his, running after him. August had not seen his son run like that in a long while.

"I'm fine!" he called out and settled his hat. He took another step into the field of corn.

"Pops! Stop! Wait!"

"The dogs've got my cane!" yelled August over his shoulder. "I can't let 'em take it! Emma wants me to have it, and I'm not gonna let some stupid mutt..." August stopped, swaying as he stood.

Behind him, Ray ducked under a rail in the fence and looked at his father, red faced and puffing.

"Pops, what in the blazes are you doing?"

"Those dogs!" said August. He shook his fists at the stalks of corn. "They took my cane! They took my cane, darn it all. Emma wanted me to have the cane so I wouldn't hurt myself! I... oh... oh dear..." He looked down at his wrists trembling in their sleeves, his shirt a couple of sizes too big for him now. They looked like a freak man's hands, like what he would have seen at a circus show when he was younger. He glanced at the bases of the corn stalks, blinking, and then back to his wax paper fingers. He shoved them into his pockets. He did not like his hands anymore. They made him afraid.

"Pops," panted Ray, looking around. "What dogs? There're no dogs here... You said they took your cane?"

August looked down at his shoes, glanced at his tie. He straightened it. "Yeah," he said, feeling like he had been caught doing something wrong. He scowled and balled up his fists in his pockets. The bones felt small, wrapped up in the shrunken flesh of his fingers.

"Pops," said Ray. He took a step toward August. "You were taking a nap on the porch is all. We thought we would let you sleep since you like to get up so early. There were no dogs. No dogs, Pops. You put down the dogs years ago, back when Mom... well... Your cane's back there hanging on your chair."

"No... no, it isn't," said August and looked back over his shoulder. He tried to point to where the dog had gone, hesitated, looked at his hand, and then tucked it back into his pocket. "Emma had me get that darned old cane so I wouldn't hurt myself."

"Yeah... She did, Pops."

The two men stood there at the edge of the corn field, the sun climbing higher but giving only a little heat.

Ray put his own hands in his own pockets. "What do you say we go back to the house, Pops? Get some breakfast." There was a jingle when Ray fiddled with some spare change.

"Sure."

Ray went over to his father and took his arm to lead him under the rails of the fence and back across the yard. As they went, he felt for August's pulse.

A bluebird trilled nearby.

When they returned to the house, a portly woman in a checkered pink dress stood at the door. Ray's wife, hands on hips, shook her head at the foolishness of old men, but August paid her no mind. He let his son's strong arms guide him to the steps of the house—the house that Emma had loved.

He took the last step back under the overhang of the porch and unhooked the cane from the arm of the chair. He stood there, not wanting to move. All around him, there was the smell of cooking and that musty smell of autumn dryness.

"What were you thinking, Pops?" asked Ray's wife, using that appellation, which was far too familiar for her.

"Honey," said Ray. He shook his head and let go of August's arm.

"He left the lantern here on the deck! The whole house could've gone up in flames—"

"Honey. Not now." Ray was a soft-spoken man. August looked up from the lantern with its blackened glass to Ray's wife.

He did not see her.

He saw Emma standing there like she had on their wedding day. She clutched her bouquet in one hand, the other hand running over the grain of the lintel. She smiled and talked to herself, marveling at the gift that August had given her. She loved it so and had walked through the empty rooms, marveling at the space. She whispered to herself of the plans for each room: *"This will be the hall, and this the kitchen with a basin, all my own, and cupboards filled with my mother's china, and this will be the stair..."* And on and on she would go, pulling at her skirts with one hand so they would not get caught on the rough lumber. She was adrift in her own bridal lace.

"Pops?"

"Mm?"

Ray touched his father's elbow.

August's eyes were a sad blue.

The door to the house stood empty, Ray's wife having gone back to turn over the sausage that he could hear popping in the pan.

"What's wrong?" asked Ray. "Is your hip hurting?"

August J. Mallard straightened his back and stamped his cane on the boards of the porch.

"I can't say, Ray." He looked out over the yard at the trees and the sky and the daytime moon that hung, spectral in the sky. "It's just... It was easier with her here. You know? It was easier to know who I was when she was here, know where I was... It was just..."

Ray put an arm around his father, and then, in a gesture that he had not given since he was a boy, he let his head rest on his father's shoulder.

"Yeah, I know, Pops," he said, voice muffled in August's oversized jacket, "I miss her, too."

FINIS.

Printed in Dunstable, United Kingdom